"Sleep if you need to."

The deep, gravelly sound of his voice made Lisa restless. Looking at him would only make it worse, make her feel those things she wasn't supposed to feel—that thread of electricity that somehow tethered them.

Lisa took off her sneakers and socks, put her ankle holster in the drawer of the bedside table and her .22 under her pillow. She lay back on the cool sheets. Sam had already turned out the dim sconce, leaving the room dark but for the light coming in through the window.

"It would be so easy to get you the kind of backup you need if you'd only tell me the whole story, Sam. You know they're going to kill you, don't you?"

Sam turned away from the window. The drapes fell back into place behind him. He took a step toward the bed. "They'

DEBRA WEBB

COLBY VS. COLBY

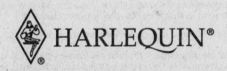

TORONTO • NEW YORK • LONDON
AMSTERDAM • PARIS • SYDNEY • HAMBURG
STOCKHOLM • ATHENS • TOKYO • MILAN • MADRID
PRAGUE • WARSAW • BUDAPEST • AUCKLAND

This book is dedicated to the City of Los Angeles,
one of the coolest places on earth. A place where
nothing is as it seems and all is as it should be.

ISBN-13: 978-0-373-69262-0
ISBN-10:   0-373-69262-5

COLBY VS. COLBY

Copyright © 2007 by Debra Webb

www.eHarlequin.com

Printed in U.S.A.

ABOUT THE AUTHOR

Debra Webb was born in Scottsboro, Alabama, to parents who taught her that anything is possible if you want it bad enough. She began writing at age nine. Eventually, she met and married the man of her dreams, and tried some other occupations, including selling vacuum cleaners, working in a factory, a day care center, a hospital and a department store. When her husband joined the military, they moved to Berlin, Germany, and Debra became a secretary in the commanding general's office. By 1985 they were back in the States, and finally moved to a small town in Tennessee, where everyone knows everyone else. With the support of her husband and two beautiful daughters, Debra took up writing again, looking to mystery and movies for inspiration. In 1998, her dream of writing for Harlequin Books came true. You can write to Debra at P.O. Box 64, Huntland, Tennessee 37345 or visit her Web site at www.debrawebb.com to find out exciting news about her next book.

Books by Debra Webb

CAST OF CHARACTERS

Sam Johnson—Former forensics expert with the LAPD. Sam knows how to keep a secret, but this one might just get him killed.

Lisa Smith—Los Angeles priority homicide detective. Lisa will do whatever it takes to find the truth.

Jim Colby—The head of the Equalizers and the son of Victoria Colby-Camp. Jim needs his mother to trust him to live his own life.

Victoria Colby-Camp—The head of the Colby Agency. Victoria wants the best for her son but she is afraid he has bitten off too much with the Equalizers.

Tasha Colby—Jim's wife and the mother of their daughter Jamie.

Spencer Anders—Former Special Forces major Anders is one of the associates at the Equalizers.

Connie Gardner—The receptionist and sometimes field operative for the Equalizers.

Renee Vaughn—A former prosecutor. The Equalizers have given her a chance to infuse some danger into her life.

Charles Sanford—Veteran LAPD priority homicide detective and Lisa's partner.

James Watts—Deceased leader of the notorious gang known as the Crew. James made a deal with Sam Johnson—is that why he's dead?

Lil Watts—Current leader of the Crew.

Buster Houston—Leader of the Nation, sworn enemy of the Crew. Buster rules by the old school.

Chapter One

Chicago's South side
Tuesday, June 4, 9:48 p.m.

"And there she goes," Jim Colby murmured as he watched the young woman dart across the dark, deserted street. "Victim number three is in position."

Sam Johnson moved his head from side to side. "How can these kids be so gullible?" He just didn't get it. With the news reporting way too often on the dirty business of runaways being sold into slavery, he just didn't see how anyone could be so oblivious to the dangers. And yet it was happening right in front of his eyes, as he sat watching from a beat-up Chevy Impala.

"Time to shut these scumbags down."

Following Jim's cue, Sam exited the passenger side. The vehicle's interior light had been disabled to ensure they weren't spotted by anyone watching the street.

Using the vehicles parked along the block as cover, Sam stole halfway up the block before pausing to survey the situation once more. Jim had taken the direct route to the office building abandoned by day and used for criminal rendezvous by night. Jim would put in a call to Chicago PD for backup as soon as he verified that all known players were in position. The Equalizers could tag and move in on this group, but the final arrests had to be made by official law enforcement personnel.

Sam hustled across the street and crouched at the rear of an SUV. If these scumbags had any spotters keeping watch, they were either asleep or blind. He steeled himself for possible confrontation and ran the last twenty yards to the northeast corner of the building inside which the despicable transaction would go down.

According to Jim, the location had once been an adoption agency. Sam found that ironic since the business taking place here most recently involved another sort of adoption: the selling of young women to the highest bidders.

Three females, ranging in age from seventeen to twenty-six, were inside. Two of those three didn't realize just yet that this was going to be one of the luckiest days of their lives. The third victim was a plant. Connie Gardner, the receptionist from the Equalizers, had agreed to step into that role. At twenty-six, Connie didn't look a day over twenty-one. Having a great body and the right look ensured she fit the profile.

Top priority was neutralizing the bad guys while maintaining the safety and well-being of the three women about to be auctioned via a private chat room on the Internet. If those scumbags inside knew what was good for them they would keep their hands off Connie. She knew how to make life miserable in a New York minute.

From his position at the main entrance, Colby tapped the mike to indicate all players were now present and visually accounted for.

Sam eased around the corner of the building, surveyed the back parking area and then hustled over to the ground-floor rear entrance. He tapped his collar mike, giving Colby the signal that he was in position. Colby would call his contact at Chicago PD and four minutes from now the world as these jerks knew it would change forever. Unfortunately, another group would take their place far too quickly.

As if to warn that the night was about to take a turn for the worst, another kind of change came earlier than Sam had anticipated. One of the hoodlums barreled out the rear entrance and ran square into him.

Sam and his startled attacker tumbled to the

ground and rolled as each attempted to gain control of the other. Sam resisted the urge to use his weapon. His enemy had dropped his weapon when they hit the ground. No need to use excessive force. His assailant went for Sam's throat. Weapon or no, the guy was determined to win this battle. At least until Sam applied just enough pressure to the carotid artery. The man slumped, unconscious. Sam shoved him off and clambered to his feet.

After tucking the lout's weapon into his waistband, Sam moved back into position at the rear exit and listened. If the unconscious chump had been sent to retrieve something, then his pals would get restless when he didn't return in a timely manner.

Sending a *complication* signal to Colby, Sam prepared to very carefully risk opening the door.

A weapon discharged inside the building, the sound shattering the silence and derailing Sam's plan. The cacophony of screaming and yelling had him rushing through the door, weapon drawn.

Two men were facedown on the floor, one was on his knees with Jim Colby's weapon boring into his sweating forehead. The two female teenagers were huddled together. Connie Gardner held a weapon she'd obviously taken from one of the men and was instructing the dudes on the floor to stay put.

Since everything appeared to be under control inside, Sam went back outside and dragged the guy who'd tackled him back inside with the others. The scumbag had started to rouse, but didn't attempt to break free.

"What happened in here?" Sam asked Connie.

She looked furious and not the least bit frightened. "They wanted to make sure we weren't wearing wires or tracking devices so they demanded we take off our clothes. Big mistake."

Sam resisted the urge to grin. Considering no one was dead he figured this team of lowlifes had gotten off easy. Connie was not one to be pushed around and she definitely knew how to use a weapon.

The wail of sirens indicated the arrival of the police. Tonight chalked up one more for the Equalizers. Chicago's finest had been trying to nail this operation for months. The man currently begging for his life in a position of humiliation in front of Jim Colby was the suspected ringleader. A few months from now, when he was in prison with guys ten times worse than him, he would be wishing Colby had put him out of his misery.

A sense of accomplishment filled Sam as he kept a bead on the others while Connie reassured the two young ladies who had thought they were coming here tonight to be extras in a movie. Their dreams had turned into nightmares, but at least they had lived to see their mistakes.

One hour later, Sam piled into the Impala with

Connie and Colby to head back to the office. It was almost midnight and he was relatively sure the silence was indication that both his colleagues were as exhausted as he was. The euphoria lingered in spite of the quiet and the fatigue. Sam genuinely liked playing the hero, no matter the risks involved. He loved his job. It beat the hell out of obsessing about the past.

As Jim Colby slowed for a changing traffic signal, he reached into his pocket and dug out his cell phone which was evidently still set to vibrate.

"Colby."

Sam didn't really pay attention to the conversation, but he did pick up on the change in tension in his boss's tone. Jim Colby was clearly not happy with the caller and/or the subject of the call.

Colby closed his phone and shoved it back into his pocket. "We have a command performance tomorrow morning," he said with a quick glance into the rearview mirror at Sam.

That couldn't be good. "The detective in charge has a problem with our statements?" Seemed a little fast to have gotten feedback, negative or otherwise, only minutes after they'd driven away from the scene of a sting operation. Usually the questions came later. Not that Sam was worried. Jim Colby might bend the hell out of the rules, but he never crossed the line, at least not more than a step or two.

"This has nothing to do with tonight's operation." Colby sent another look in Sam's direction. "We have an appointment at eight sharp at the Colby Agency. Victoria needs to see us."

Now Sam understood the irritation.

Jim Colby's *mom* had called.

Checking up on her son had gotten to be a regular routine for the lady. And judging by the muscle flexing in Colby's jaw, it was not appreciated.

The real question was, why would she want to see Sam?

Colby Agency
Wednesday, June 5, 8:00 a.m.

JIM COLBY WAS twenty-eight years old. He was married with a daughter. He had opened the doors to his own cutting-edge firm just this year. The Equalizers were swiftly making a name for themselves as the place to go when all else failed.

He had faced death on more occasions than he could recall, and he'd doled it out far more times than any man would want to admit. The possibility of having his wife or child hurt was the one thing in this world that scared him; otherwise he was fearless. And yet here he sat, with dread tying his gut in knots as he waited for his own mother to call him into her private office.

Not that he was afraid of his mother; he wasn't.

But her need to protect him, to ensure his every move was cautiously executed was, frankly, making him nuts. Since the birth of his daughter, his mother's hovering had only gotten worse.

"Jim."

He looked up to see Mildred, his mother's personal assistant and longtime friend, approaching the sitting area outside Victoria's office. Pushing to his feet, he propped a smile into place. "Mildred."

"Victoria is ready to see you now." She directed an acknowledging nod at Sam Johnson as he stood. "If you don't mind waiting, Mr. Johnson, it will only be a few more minutes before you can go in, as well."

Jim felt his gaze narrow with suspicion. What was Victoria up to? He sent Johnson a "beats me" look as the man resumed his seat.

Mildred led the way to the door on the other side of the small waiting area and opened it. "Let me know if you change your mind about coffee."

Jim didn't respond, his entire attention already focused on the room beyond the door Mildred had just opened. The setting was a little generic, not at all his mother's usual elegant style, but this building was only temporary office space. The agency's new home was still under construction.

He walked in, instantly feeling his tension escalate to the next level. The Colby Agency had that effect on him; always had. He imagined most anyone who entered the inner sanctum of the head of the Colby Agency—temporary or not—experienced the same. For more than a quarter of a century, the Colby Agency had stood head and shoulders above the rest as the most prestigious private investigation agency in Chicago, perhaps in the whole country. Jim admired his mother and all she had done.

"Jim, thank you for coming."

"Victoria," he acknowledged.

His mother indicated the wingchair to his left. "Please have a seat." She settled into the leather executive chair behind her desk.

It wasn't until Jim moved around the chair she'd designated that he saw the other person already seated in the room. Female. Blond hair, brown eyes. Thirtyish. Posture rigid. Gaze assessing. A cop.

The woman extended her hand. "Hello, Mr. Colby."

Yep. Definitely a cop. She had that formal bearing, that watchful eye.

Jim pumped the lady's hand once then looked to his mother for an explanation.

"Please make yourself comfortable, Jim. This is Detective Lisa Smith. She and I will explain everything."

He lowered himself into the chair, analyzing the three words uttered by the woman seated next to him when she'd shaken his hand. "West Coast?" he asked, turning his attention to Detective Smith.

"L.A.," she confirmed.

Now he got the picture.

"Jim, Detective Smith flew in to Chicago yesterday. She came directly to my office with some concerns of which I believe you need to be aware."

Major patience was required to keep his temper in check. He'd already gotten the picture. "What kind of concerns?"

"You may or may not know, Mr. Colby," Detective Smith began in that careful tone cops used when they intended to tell you something that would actually tell you nothing at all, "but the three men who murdered Sam Johnson's fiancée allegedly belonged to a notorious L.A. gang known as the Crew."

He met her gaze with one that cut her no slack. He understood exactly why she was here, and he didn't like it at all. "I am very much aware of the kind of thugs who raped and murdered Anna Denali. The bastards deserved what they got, and if you're here looking for conclusions as to whether or not Sam Johnson had anything to do with their executions then you've come to the wrong man."

The detective didn't back down. "I'm not here for your conclusions, Mr. Colby. I'm here for the truth," she said frankly. "Sam's name has come up in recent gangland rumblings. There's still a contract out on him, and someone has recently decided to provide the necessary motivation to see that it's fulfilled."

"And," Jim countered, "you wouldn't mind clearing up that unsolved case sitting on the corner of your desk in the process. Isn't that right, Detective?"

Detective Smith's gaze held his, but he saw the faintest flicker of indecision.

"Jim," Victoria cut through the mounting tension, "Detective Smith's first obligation is to protect. That's why she has come to us rather than launch an official investigation of her own."

Jim's attention never deviated from the detective. "Really? Or maybe your lieutenant didn't think there was enough evidence to launch an official investigation so you're on your own."

Another glimmer of doubt told him he'd hit the nail on the head.

"I considered coming to you first," Detective Smith said. "Now I'm glad I listened to my instincts. You obviously can't see beyond your own uninformed deductions regarding a case about which you've heard only one totally unobjective side."

Jim laughed softly, but there wasn't a damned thing pleasant about it, any more than there was about the irritation churning inside him. "You would be correct, Detective." He stood, leveled a firm stare on Victoria. "I'm quite certain you can decide what cases your agency should take without any assistance from me. This meeting is over."

He turned his back and headed for the door. Right now was not a good time to speculate what the hell Victoria had meant calling him here, much less taking this pointless case. He'd form his conclusions when he'd cooled off and could think more rationally.

"Jim."

Hesitating wasn't something he would have done in the past. But there he stood at the door, making that hopeful pause…giving Victoria the benefit of the doubt. He needed her to trust him. This meeting, the detective's presence, screamed of distrust and doubt.

"I'm taking this case," Victoria said, "for *you*."

Fury kindled, diminishing the hope and amping up his already soaring tension. He turned to face his mother. "I don't need protecting, Victoria. I can handle anything that comes my way. You of all people should be aware of just how well I can do that."

Victoria didn't falter. He hadn't expected she would. "I would like to offer a compromise."

"What kind of compromise?" He shouldn't stand for this…but she was his mother. Changing her mind would take nothing short of a presidential veto.

That Detective Smith kept quiet told Jim hat she and Victoria had already discussed the likelihood of this reaction and that the two had agreed on this so-called compromise. That only annoyed him all the more. Unreasonably so.

"The police aren't going to investigate the threat to Sam," Victoria suggested, "until someone has actually committed a crime against him, and that might be too late. I'm certain you don't want Sam hurt any more than he already has been."

That much was true. Jim dropped his hand away from the door. "So, you're going to look into the case." He didn't need her to spell it out. The Colby Agency took cases like this all the time. But this was Jim's associate. The case should be his. It should be handled by the Equalizers.

"Actually, one of my investigators is going to work with Detective Smith," Victoria explained. "Detective Smith knows the territory and the facts surrounding what happened to Sam's fiancée better than anyone. Her knowledge and contacts are crucial."

"Why send one of your investigators?" Jim countered, determination and some amount of arrogance nudging him to push the issue. "As invaluable as Detective Smith's knowledge of the case and her contacts might be, Sam Johnson's would be even better. This case should be his. He's the one with the most to lose."

Even from across the room he noted the slight shift in his mother's posture as she said, "He's too close. The case is too personal for him."

Jim resisted the impulse to laugh. "We both know

that rule is only applicable in theory. It has no place in real life, otherwise Detective Smith wouldn't be involved in this case."

Victoria held his gaze for several seconds. Whatever she said next, she could not deny his assertion.

"Perhaps you're right. Why don't we call in Sam and see what kind of compromise we can reach?"

Jim didn't miss the way the detective tensed at the suggestion. Interesting. If she was on the up-and-up she had nothing to hide.

"You have a problem with that, Detective Smith?" He shifted the conversation back to the lady from L.A.

She turned fully to meet his gaze. "Absolutely not."

"Good." Jim looked back to Victoria then. "This is the only right way to do this. I don't think we want to go down that other road."

Victoria nodded once in acknowledgment of the line he'd drawn. Jim opened the door and gestured for Johnson to join him.

As he entered the room, Jim said, "Johnson, I'm sure you know Detective Smith from L.A."

Johnson stopped in the middle of the room. His gaze collided with the detective's.

Smith rose from her chair. "Hello, Mr. Johnson."

The tension that rippled through Jim's associate was more than just surprise. There was something between him and the detective. Something more than the ugly history of the homicide investigation.

"Detective Smith," Johnson said before glancing over at Jim.

"Detective Smith has come all the way from L.A.," Jim noted, working hard to keep the sarcasm out of his tone as he brought his associate up to speed, "because she believes there is some threat to your life."

"There's talk," Smith explained, "that the Crew is planning a hit on you."

Sam digested that information for three or four beats. "And you felt compelled to deliver that message in person?"

Definitely something between these two. Jim saw it in his associate's posture and heard it in his voice.

Smith blinked once, twice. "I think it's past time we got to the bottom of what really happened. That way maybe we can stop this before someone else has to die."

"The truth is," Johnson said with a bluntness that held everyone in the room silent, "your department couldn't care less if I die. This isn't about helping me, and you know it. It's about solving a case that baffled L.A.'s finest, and I don't mean my fiancée's murder."

Jim had to give Detective Smith credit, she held her ground. Her navy slacks and pale blue blouse were pristine, not a wrinkle, and her poise was nothing less than professional. When she spoke, her voice was strong and steady.

"My partner would like nothing better than to nail you, that's true," she admitted, "but I don't share his theories on what really happened. What I do believe in is the truth. I think it's time we knew what that was." And then she made a major strategical error. "I also think you're way overdue to stop running from the past."

Sam Johnson executed an about-face and stalked out of the room.

Jim didn't follow, but he did offer the detective a bit of sage advice. "If you want his cooperation, it's best not to insult him until he's committed."

Smith squared her shoulders. "I'll talk to him."

To Jim's surprise, she took off after Johnson. He had to give her credit; the lady was definitely determined.

"I hope you understand why I'm doing this, Jim."

Jim studied Victoria for a bit before saying exactly what was on his mind. "You're the one who needs to understand. I'm not that little boy who vanished twenty years ago. You have to stop punishing yourself for that, Victoria. It wasn't your fault. You need to come to terms with the reality that I'm a grown man. I survived twenty years in hell without you. I don't need you looking over my shoulder now."

He didn't want to hurt her, but he had to get that through to her…somehow.

Chapter Two

Sam cleared the stairs leading down to the second floor of the Colby Agency's temporary home. One more floor and he'd hit the lobby and be out of there.

"Johnson, wait!"

He hesitated on the landing halfway between the first and second floors and closed his eyes for five seconds in an attempt to calm the rage simmering inside him before he said something he would regret. Detective Lisa Smith had no business showing up here. Damn it!

"What do you want?" he demanded when she hesitated one step above him. What did she hope to accomplish by coming here? He was just beginning to enjoy his new life. He didn't need the past barging in.

"I want the truth, Johnson. You can't keep running away from it." She rested her hand on the railing and took the last step down to stand toe to toe with him. "As long as I have a breath left in me I'm going to keep haunting you. You should know that by now."

Oh, yeah, he knew. He'd gone through months and months of hell because of her and her partner. The last four months of long-awaited peace weren't nearly enough to banish those dark days.

He looked directly into her eyes, let her see the resolve in his. "You're wasting your time, Detective Smith. You won't ever know what happened. You can dog my every step for the rest of my life. It's not going to work." A ragged, involuntary exhale reminded him that he'd been holding his breath.

"Then we have a problem, Sam," she said with a fortitude that matched his own. "Because it's going to take both of us to stop what's going down back home even as we speak." She lifted her chin and ratcheted up the warning in her eyes. "And I'm not going back to L.A. without you."

He leaned closer, heard her breath hitch at the un-expected move. "No, Detective, *we* don't have a problem. *You* have a problem." He knew his civil rights forward and back. No way could she make him go back without a court order. If she'd had one, they wouldn't be having this discussion right now. She would have arrived with her partner and all would have been handled swiftly and by the book.

As if he hadn't said a word, she took another shot

at convincing him. "Lil Watts has issued a new contract on you. You'll be lucky to survive the week. No one close to you will be safe. Maybe you've forgotten how these guys work."

Sam looked away, remembered terror slithered beneath his skin in spite of his best efforts to suppress any and all emotion. He still had a sister in L.A. Parents. None of whom understood his decision to leave…could never know his reason. The words he refused to utter aloud stuck in his throat. His family was supposed to be safe as long as he stayed away. That was the deal.

"When did things change?" His voice was bitter, brittle, as he leveled his attention on the detective once more.

"About two weeks ago." Her eyes told him she wanted to back up a step, but she stayed put. "I guess you didn't hear about it. The Man is dead. Murdered. Lil Watts took over. He's shaking things up. Every damned gang in L.A. is restless. I think he wants to set his own precedents. Make himself look superior by having his long-awaited vengeance on you—the one that got away."

Sam knew the gang members weren't the only ones nervous. The riots of 1992 hadn't been forgotten by anyone who'd lived through them. She was right. He hadn't heard. He'd stopped watching the news a long time ago. But her revelation certainly explained why she was here. The Man had made the deal with Sam, and he was dead.

That meant one thing: open season on Sam Johnson and anyone he cared about.

"What's the standing order?" There would be specifics. It wouldn't be enough just to make him dead. Lil Watts liked pumping up the drama and the gore. Like Napoleon, his small stature dictated that he constantly attempt to make up for what he lacked in size. He wouldn't rest until he'd made a circus act out of the situation and proved just how big and powerful he was to the world he now represented.

"Your head," she said bluntly, "delivered to him on the proverbial platter. He chose six of his most devoted followers—whichever one brings him what he wants gets to be his right-hand man."

Now there was some heavy incentive. A scuzz-ball's wet dream.

"So, basically, I'm a dead man."

Those brown eyes searched his before she nodded, her expression grim.

If Sam was nowhere to be found, the more am-bitious and intelligent of the chosen hunters would go for his unsuspecting family. He didn't need the good detective to tell him that.

"What about Sanford?" Detective Charles San-ford had hated allowing Sam to walk away. He'd taken it badly when he hadn't been able to prove

Sam's involvement in the murders of those who had killed Anna. Sanford hadn't given Sam a minute's peace as long as he had remained in Los Angeles.

"In a nutshell," she replied, "he's hoping to be the one to ID your remains." A weary sigh escaped her. "He doesn't know I'm here. The whole division thinks I'm on vacation in Mexico."

Sanford would love nothing better than to dance on Sam's grave. No surprise there. The truly startling idea was that *she* was here. That she'd warned him what was going down. "If your partner finds out you lied to him he's not going to be happy." Sanford wasn't the type to forgive this kind of perceived betrayal, no matter if justice was Smith's primary motive, and Sam wasn't entirely sure about that. Sounded a little too simple to him.

"I don't intend for him to find out," she countered, the frankness in her expression credible.

He got the picture now. "You think we can do this under the radar?"

Another of those barely discernible nods. "We'll go in dark. Keep a low profile while we try and neutralize this situation before anyone gets hurt. If we prove you weren't involved in the murders, assuming you weren't, then Watts should back off."

"Impossible." She was out of her mind. If this was her way of getting him to come clean about what really happened, she could forget it.

"It's the only way I can help you." For the first time since she'd arrived, he saw a flicker of trepidation in her eyes. "You have to trust me, *Sam.*"

He ignored the new kind of tension that filtered through him when she used his first name like that… like she cared. He couldn't afford any soft feelings where this woman was concerned. "What you're suggesting, Detective—" his gaze bored into hers "—will not set me free. It will only get us killed."

"You're dead, anyway."

He couldn't argue with that. "There are far better ways to achieve a promotion, Smith." If she wanted to make the next pay grade she should focus on kissing up to the brass, not digging around in cold cases that would get her six feet under.

Her one hand resting on the railing, she plowed the fingers of the other through her hair as if her patience had thinned. "I told you—"

"I know what you told me," he cut in. "Don't play games with me, Detective. Give it to me straight. If I'm going back to L.A. with you, I at least need to know you're not a head case. I have no desire to go dark with a cop who's suicidal."

Well, hell, he'd really messed up now. He'd given her that inch she wanted so desperately. He'd admitted that he was going back to L.A. It wasn't as if he had a choice. When had his brain staged a mutiny and decided he was going with her?

This time when she met his eyes there was no trepidation. That unyielding determination was back, full force. Maybe even had a little anger in the mix. "I want to help you get your life back…for real."

That tug he hadn't felt in months—not since the last time they'd stood this close—had him fighting the need to lean closer…to taste the grim line of those lush lips. Oh, yeah. Ten minutes around her and he'd already lost his grip on reality. He had to be out of his mind to even consider what she was proposing.

He was a fool, that was for sure.

Sam drew back a step, mentally shook off the too-intense moment. There wasn't any going back now. "We should go back to Victoria's office and work out the particulars."

"Does this mean you're going back to L.A. with me?"

If she was surprised at his decision, she kept the reaction carefully concealed behind that inflexible cop demeanor she'd yanked back into place.

"It means I'm going back. Whether I go with you or not is yet to be seen."

He walked around her and headed up the stairwell.

It wasn't like he had a choice. He couldn't let Watts carry out his vengeance on his family.

Going back to L.A. was the last thing he'd ever expected to do.

Ironically it probably would be the last thing he ever did.

LISA SMITH couldn't take the first step upward. Not yet. His answer had shocked her. She hadn't expected him to agree to go back to L.A. quite so easily. Not in a million years, actually.

A dozen steps up he abruptly stopped and turned to her. "You coming?"

Heat rushed up her neck and across her cheeks. If he noted her hesitation, thought for one second she couldn't handle this, he would refuse to cooperate. She knew the kind of man she was dealing with here. "Yeah. I'm right behind you." She took the steps two at a time until she'd reached the one just below him.

Instead of giving her his back and resuming his climb upward, he studied her…too close. She banished all emotion. Stared right back at him. Whatever he was thinking, she wouldn't have him reading her. She remembered all too well just how good he was at that particular skill.

When he decided the intimidation wasn't going to work, he turned forward and headed back up to Victoria Colby-Camp's office. Lisa didn't draw a deep breath until they were inside that neutral territory. Victoria had agreed to help her. That put her on Lisa's side. Strange, that decision also seemed to pit her directly against her own son. Lisa wasn't sure of the story there.

Jim Colby still stood in front of his mother's

desk, looking annoyed at the whole situation. Victoria remained calm and as regal-looking as when Lisa had first met her yesterday afternoon.

"I have to go back to L.A. and handle this," Sam said to Jim Colby. "There really isn't any other way."

"I can send Anders with you," Jim suggested. "You'll need backup."

Sam shook his head. Lisa had known he would do that.

"I have to do this alone."

Lisa held up both hands stop-sign fashion. "We do this my way, Johnson. I'm the one with the badge." No way was she going to have him going vigilante. Again. He had to understand who was in charge, here and now. Now that she knew he was going back, she could afford to push the boundaries a little. The glare he pointed in her direction told her what he thought of that idea.

"I would much prefer," Victoria interrupted, maneuvering easily through the thick tension radiating between Lisa and Johnson, "sending one of my investigators at least in a support capacity."

"Support would be helpful, as long as there's no question who's in charge." Lisa looked from Victoria to her son, Jim Colby. Both were determined to help, but she needed him to be onboard with her. Jim Colby kept whatever he was thinking to himself.

Johnson, however, did not. He moved his head firmly from side to side. "No one else gets involved. The only way to do this is by slipping into that world, the less fanfare the better. It's too risky to drag anyone else into the situation."

Lisa couldn't argue the validity of that particular point, but backup could make the difference between success and failure. She couldn't call on anyone in Homicide for support of any nature. If they figured out what she was up to, the chief would have her shield. Not to mention that Chuck would probably request a new partner.

"We'll need logistical support," Lisa argued, infusing as much logic into her tone as possible. "We can't go under deep cover and handle any necessary logistics at the same time."

Johnson appeared to consider her assertion. Good. She'd made him think. The operation they were talking about was extremely dicey at best. Any and all help behind the scenes that didn't come from LAPD would be beneficial.

"All right. Logistical support and that's it. No one goes in except me."

There he went again. "And me," she reminded, setting him straight.

He looked away, gave his attention to his boss. "I need to make arrangements for my family." His sister was ten years his junior. She still lived with his parents while she completed her doctorate at UCLA.

"I'll send two of my investigators to serve as security," Victoria offered. "I have several who are the absolute best to be found."

"Anders will provide logistical support," Jim Colby said to Sam, choosing not to comment on his mother's offer. "Anything you need, you let him know. He's been in far worse places than L.A.'s gang world."

Johnson said to Lisa, "Spencer Anders is former Special Forces. He spent most of his time in the Middle East. He could handle this with his eyes closed."

"Good." She didn't mention that she already knew Anders was former military. She'd run a complete background check on the Equalizers the day Johnson went to work there. "There's a flight that leaves at three this afternoon. We could be on it," Lisa suggested. The sooner they were on their way the better, in fact. She didn't want him having any extra time to reconsider.

"That'll work," he agreed, though it didn't sound as if his heart was in the decision.

"Let's use the agency jet," Victoria offered as she pushed out of her chair. "That way the two of you can brief the others en route, and equipment transport won't be a problem. Airport security makes getting across country with the necessities for an assignment like this nearly impossible."

Victoria was right. A private aircraft would make travel considerably less complicated for all involved. Excellent idea or not, Lisa couldn't help noticing the increasing tension in Jim Colby. His posture grew even more rigid and his jaw tightened to the point that a muscle repeatedly contracted there. Apparently, he was not pleased with what he presumed to be Victoria's interference. When running that background check, Lisa had learned that Jim Colby was Victoria's son. Evidently, Victoria had remarried since her surname was now Colby-Camp. Maybe that was part of the problem. Whatever. Lisa was no shrink, but her gut instinct told her that there was an explosion coming between these two.

Or maybe Victoria was unhappy that her son had started his own firm rather going into the family business. Lisa had wondered at that. Evidently Jim had drawn a line in the sand, professionally speaking, and Victoria just kept crossing it. A standoff, Colby versus Colby. Lisa would just as soon not be around when those two reached their breaking points. And it was coming, fast, that much was as plain as day.

Jim turned to Johnson. "We should get the communications equipment together. I don't want you out of touch with Anders."

"And fire power," Johnson added.

"I'll instruct the pilot to prepare," Victoria said to no one in particular, though Lisa suspected what she wanted was for her son to acknowledge her act of support.

"Can we be ready to go by three?" Lisa looked from one man to the other. She recognized that Victoria needed certain information, starting with takeoff time.

Johnson shifted his attention to her, though reluctantly so. "Three will give us plenty of time."

Jim Colby nodded. "We'll rendezvous at the airfield at two-thirty," he said to Victoria.

His comment felt like a dismissal to both her and Victoria, but Lisa wasn't going anywhere without Sam Johnson. No way was she going to risk him taking off on her and doing this on his own.

"I don't see any reason to hang around here," she said with a glance in Victoria's direction. "I can drop my rental off and join the two of you for preparations," she said to Jim Colby. "If—" this was the tricky part "—Johnson doesn't mind giving me a ride from the rental car agency."

Johnson stared straight at her. For three beats she was certain he was going to say no.

"I can do that."

He didn't want to, his body language shouted that message loud and clear, but for some reason he didn't turn her down.

Lisa offered her hand across Victoria's desk. "Thank you for your help, Mrs. Colby-Camp."

Victoria shook her hand. "I'll see you this afternoon, Detective Smith. I'm certain that we can find the truth you're looking for and neutralize this volatile situation for Mr. Johnson."

Hoping like hell she was right, Lisa turned to Sam Johnson. "Are you ready?"

To Jim Colby, Johnson said, "I'll see you back at the office."

Colby confirmed with a nod. "I'll just finish up here."

With Johnson right behind her, Lisa left Victoria's office without a backward glance. She could feel the tension mounting once more, pushing the air out of the room. Mother and son weren't finished by any means.

The trip down the two flights of stairs was made without conversation this time and with every bit as much tension as before. They'd reached the parking lot before Johnson said a word to her.

"Which rental agency?" he asked without so much as a glance at her.

"Budget."

"I'll meet you there."

She wanted to say no. To tell him that she'd rather stay close behind him or have him follow her.

"Okay." At least she knew what kind of car he drove and his license plate number. She'd just have to keep him in her line of sight.

Lisa headed for her rental, keeping an eye on Sam Johnson as he strode toward his own sedan. She got into her car and started the engine. The opportunity to hit the street at the same time he did wasn't possible, but she did fall in three cars behind him.

She gripped the steering wheel in a death lock as she waited for an opportunity to maneuver closer to his black sedan. A stop light caught her after he'd passed through it.

"Damn!"

Her heart thudding in her chest, she waited for the green. Her foot instinctively shifted from the brake to the accelerator the instant the light changed. She'd never catch him now.

The cell phone in her pocket vibrated. Not taking her eyes off the back of Johnson's car, she dug out her phone and took a breath.

"Smith."

"Hey, Smith, where the hell are you?"

Lisa's pulse skittered. Her partner, Charles Sanford.

"I'm…headed to a spa appointment," she lied. "Where the hell are you?"

She cut right, edging between two cars, which left only one between her and Johnson.

"I figured you'd still be in bed. You're supposed to be partying, hanging out in the bars all night. Isn't that what singles do when they go to Cozumel?"

She glanced at the digital clock on the dash— 9:20 a.m. Two hours earlier in L.A.

"I had to take the first appointment of the morning to get this particular masseur. He's supposed to be the best." She bit her lip and hoped he'd go for the lie.

"Oh-ho, I see how it is. Well, enjoy. I just wanted to check in and make sure you were behaving yourself."

"Thanks, Chuck. I'll see you next week."

Lisa closed the phone and slid it back into her pocket. Was her partner suspicious? She couldn't be sure. She'd given him no reason to be…but he was no fool. He'd been at this a whole lot longer than she had. He knew she was obsessing over the news about Johnson. In fact, she'd used that as her excuse for the abrupt vacation. The timing had worked out perfectly. Her parents were away on vacation with friends, as well, so she didn't have to worry about them calling to check up on her.

Still, her story might not be enough for her partner.

Pushing her partner's call aside, she changed lanes, tried to get behind Sam's car. She'd almost caught up with him. As she moved closer, a look at the license plate told her she'd made a mistake at some point since leaving the Colby Agency parking lot.

This wasn't Johnson's car.

Where was he?

There was no other vehicle matching his for as far as she could see.

With no other choice, she drove to the rental agency and parked. No sign of Sam Johnson in the lot.

Just her luck. Less than an hour after coming face-to-face with him again and he'd lied to her already.

So much for finding the truth.

Chapter Three

Sam watched Lisa Smith climb out of her rental car and survey the lot. She was looking for him. He shouldn't keep her guessing like this, but he needed to be sure of her motives. He'd played a little switch-and-bait with her, falling in between a couple of other black sedans and then abruptly making an exit while she followed the others. Even with that one traffic signal to his advantage, he could only assume she'd been distracted, otherwise he wasn't sure he would have fooled her so easily.

He'd taken a shortcut to the rental agency and parked where he could watch her arrive.

When she walked out of the rental office, an overnight bag in her hand, and took another long look around the lot, he decided to put her out of her misery. He backed out of the parking slot where he'd waited, then pulled up right in front of her.

She tried to act as if she weren't surprised as she

stowed her bag in the back, then slid into the passenger seat, but he knew better.

"Did you get an unexpected call?" he ventured as he merged into the traffic on the street.

Her startled glance in his direction gave him his answer. He'd been guessing, of course. But a cell phone call was the most likely culprit whenever a driver got distracted. Since she didn't have any passengers, hadn't been eating while driving and there hadn't been any traffic incidents to vie for her attention, then the cell phone was the probable candidate. He'd gotten away from her too easily to believe that one traffic signal had done the trick. This lady was trained in surveillance.

"Or maybe you made one," he went on when she couldn't decide how to answer. "Maybe to let your partner know how and when we were arriving."

The line of her jaw tightened. She didn't have to be looking at him for him to sense her anger. He'd ticked her off by suggesting she was keeping something from him. That she didn't deny his charges didn't bode well. The detective was hiding something, it seemed.

"Detective Sanford called," she said crisply, maintaining that steady watch on the traffic in front of their car.

"Did you give him an update on me?" He should

have known that she wouldn't be working alone. The cop mentality was pair oriented.

"I told him I was on my way to a spa appointment." She looked at him then. "He thinks I'm in Cozumel on vacation."

Sam fixed his attention on the street as he maneuvered through midmorning traffic. "If I find out you're lying to me—"

"You won't."

Instead of driving directly to the office, he turned in the direction of his place. He might as well pack a bag and check the aquarium. Once preparation was underway back at the office, he didn't want to have to break away for anything as menial as grabbing his toothbrush. He'd driven a dozen or so blocks before she spoke up. He hadn't expected to get that far.

"Where are we going?"

"My place." He took the next left. "I'm sure you already know the address."

She didn't bother denying his charge. He imagined that she knew all there was to know about him except the details of why and how the three scumbags who murdered Anna were executed.

He couldn't really hold that against her. He'd done his research on her, as well as her partner, not long after his fiancée was murdered. At the time, he'd considered it his job to know if the cops on the case were up to snuff.

"I know a few things myself. Lisa Marie Smith," he said out loud, mostly to unnerve her. "Thirty-one, born in San Diego, graduated Berkley with a degree in criminology. Made detective just over five years ago, much to the annoyance of your male peers. Assigned to homicide one month later. No family in L.A. Never been married. One dog."

She continued her steady gaze out the windshield. "The dog died. Old age. I'd had him since I was in high school."

"That's a shame." He slowed the car and took a right turn. "I'm sure you miss him." He'd had a dog once. But the animal had gotten so attached to Anna that he'd literally grieved himself to death after her murder. Sam had decided after that he'd stick with fish.

Anna. He didn't say or think her name very often. He banished the images that immediately attempted to intrude on his thoughts. Anytime he did he was sorry for it. She was gone. There was nothing he could do to bring her back. Her parents hated him, held him responsible. He couldn't blame them. He was responsible. It was his fault Anna had died.

"Nice place," Smith said as he made the final turn.

His thoughts drifted back to the present with her comment. He parked in the driveway of his Oak Park home. The price he'd gotten for his Hollywood Hills home would have bought something much larger and in the ritziest market available in Chicago, but he hadn't been looking for glamour or square footage.

This place gave him the peace and quiet he needed.

By the time he'd gotten out and rounded the hood, she had already emerged from the passenger side. He led the way up the walk and to the door.

"Seems quiet," she remarked.

"It is." Since school was out for the summer, there would be a little more excitement around the neighborhood throughout the day. Otherwise the neatly manicured lawns were clear of clutter and people during the morning hours.

First thing, he checked the aquarium and filled up the automatic feeder. He could be gone for two weeks and not have to worry. Fish didn't need to be walked or boarded at the kennel. Didn't need baths or any particular attention. Just a clean tank and food.

Uncomplicated. That was his new motto.

Smith stood in the middle of his living room looking around. He hadn't bothered with any decorating and, admittedly, the furniture left something to be desired. But he didn't spend much time here so he didn't actually care. He'd sold his house in California fully furnished. Too many memories to bring any of the stuff with him.

"Have a seat. I'll only be a few minutes."

His new home had two bedrooms, one he'd

turned into an office. That was the one part of his past he'd kept, his research books. As a forensics scientist, he'd used reference materials daily. So far he hadn't really needed them in his new job, but it didn't hurt to have them around.

He grabbed a duffel from his closet and stuffed it with two changes of dark-colored clothes, gloves and the necessary toiletries. He threw in a mini flashlight and a small first-aid kit.

"You kept your reference books."

Sam turned at the sound of her voice. She stood in the open doorway, but made no move to enter his bedroom. That she'd peeked into his home office didn't surprise him. A cop didn't stop being a cop just because she or he wasn't on official duty.

"I did." He zipped the duffel and lifted it off the unmade bed. "I'm ready."

"You didn't keep any pictures of her?"

She stayed in that doorway almost as if she intended to have her answers before she let him pass. Evidently she'd already had herself a better look around than he'd realized.

"No." He'd sold or put away everything, except the books, related to the past.

"You shouldn't pretend she didn't exist."

If those brown eyes hadn't looked so sincere, he might have considered that she was baiting him, but he could see that she was serious.

"She's dead. She doesn't care what I pretend." He moved toward the door, expecting the nosy detective to step out of the way. She didn't.

"That's how you're dealing with it?"

What the hell did she want from him? The last time he'd spoken with Detective Lisa Smith she'd been convinced he'd killed three men in cold blood. Did she believe she could get close to him like this and find that truth she wanted so badly to know?

"Let's get one thing straight."

She still didn't back off, just looked directly into his eyes.

"My personal life is off-limits. It's none of your business. End of story."

"Strange," she said with a puzzled expression. "I thought this whole thing was personal. Three members of a notorious gang killed your fiancée, then ended up dead a short time after. Lil Watts wants you dead. Sanford wants you on death row. What part of that do you feel *isn't* personal?"

He stepped directly into her personal space and cranked up the irritation in his tone when he spoke. "This is never going to work, Smith."

"Probably not," she agreed without a glimmer of trepidation as she stared up at him. "But I don't see any point in pretending I don't want answers or that how you're dealing with the past doesn't matter."

"Stick to the facts related to the case," he ordered.

"We're not friends. We've never been friends. How I'm dealing with life in general isn't your concern."

She pivoted on her heel and walked back into the living room. He watched her go, tamped his emotions back down to a more manageable place.

If he got even an inkling that she was working a scam on him, this liaison was over.

For now he had no choice but to go along with her. He'd been out of touch with life in L.A. for more than four months. He needed the detective to get him back up to speed. Then he might just have to break out on his own. That option would be in her best interest, anyway. If she hung around him too long she would likely end up dead.

The Offices of the Equalizers
1:45 p.m.

"THAT SHOULD COVER IT." Jim Colby shuffled the stack of reports they had just gone over. The reports included everything from seven-day weather forecasts to topographical maps of Los Angeles County.

The communication links were wireless and the tracking devices were state-of-the-art. Spencer Anders would serve as backup. Sam wasn't exactly sure how that would work in real time, but he had to say he was glad for the support as long as Anders stayed out of the line of fire.

"You have a question, Detective Smith?"

Sam looked from Jim Colby to Smith. She'd picked up one of the reports from his stack and appeared to be studying it.

"I'm wondering how a private citizen in another state was able to get hold of an arrest record." She dropped the report back onto the stack. "I don't think I could have gotten it any faster."

Renee Vaughn, another of Sam's colleagues here at the Equalizers, stood. "I'm a former assistant prosecutor," she said with a quick smile. "I know the ropes, Detective. However, if you take issue with our under-the-table contacts, I would suggest you take it up with the boss." She aimed a wider smile at Jim Colby.

Smith held up both hands. "I have no issues with your tactics. I'm impressed, that's all."

The tension in the room reduced significantly.

Spencer Anders grabbed a gear bag. "We should head for the airfield. Wheels up in one hour."

Sam picked up the remaining bag. "Let's do it."

LISA CLIMBED into the backseat of the SUV belonging to Jim Colby.

"The pilot's sitting on ready," Jim announced as he closed his phone and started the vehicle. "Victoria has Brett Call and Jeff Battles rendezvousing with us there."

Lisa wondered why Jim called his mother by her

first name. Perhaps it was an effort to keep the conversation on a strictly professional level. But it felt like more than that. The tension she'd noted between the two went deeper than a need to maintain professionalism.

The drive to the private airfield utilized by the Colby Agency took just over half an hour. Spencer Anders and Sam Johnson kept a running dialogue regarding the gear they carried and the possible technical problems they might encounter. Lisa didn't mind that they left her out of the discussion loop. More than once she noticed Jim Colby watching her in the rearview mirror. She'd been with Sam Johnson since he'd learned of her presence in Chicago, so she was relatively sure the two men hadn't talked privately. Maybe she was being paranoid, but she had the feeling that Jim Colby was suspicious of her.

Then again, his conclusions about her could have more to do with Victoria taking her case than with anything else. Time would tell, she supposed.

Once at the airfield, Jim followed the signs to Hangar 3. Another SUV, black like the one belonging to Jim, waited. The Lear jet sat on the tarmac, fueled and ready for takeoff.

Lisa unloaded as soon as the SUV was parked. She joined the others at the rear and handled her own bag. Both Anders and Sam carried their personal bags, as well as a gear bag. There was more they'd have to come back for, the additional weapons and more sensitive communications equipment.

As they strode toward the aircraft, the occupants of the other SUV emerged. Victoria Colby-Camp and three men, members of her staff, Lisa presumed.

"Detective Smith," Victoria said as she approached, "this is Ian Michaels, my second in command, and investigators Brett Call and Jeff Battles."

Lisa shook hands with each of the men. Ian Michaels had the dark, mysterious look of a true spymaster. Jeff Battles would blend right in on any West Coast beach with his surfer-guy tan and blond hair. Brett Call had the broad shoulders of a football linebacker, but the red hair and freckles gave him the appearance of the boy next door. Judging by what she'd learned about the Colby Agency in her research, there was probably a great deal more than met the eye with these gentlemen.

"Don't hesitate to call on Jeff and Brett," Victoria reminded Lisa. "The Colby Agency's every asset is at your disposal."

"Anything you need," Jim Colby interjected with a look first at Lisa then at Sam, "I'm one phone call away."

Something like fear flashed in Victoria's eyes, puzzling Lisa for a moment, then she recognized it for what it was. Concern for her son's well-being.

Lisa considered the tall, well-muscled man in question. It didn't make sense for Victoria to worry on that level. The guy certainly looked as if he could take care of himself in most any situation. But there was something more, beyond the obvious. Lisa had noticed it before.

"Sam," Victoria said, drawing his attention to her. "Brett and Jeff are prepared to follow whatever instructions you feel appropriate for the protection of your family. I would suggest that Jeff tag around the university with your sister. He fits the proper profile."

"Those decisions will be made en route," Jim pointed out. Though his tone was cool and calm there was no mistaking his insistence on maintaining the lead.

Glad when the time came, Lisa was the first to go aboard the aircraft.

"Good afternoon, Detective Smith. I'm Race Payne, I'm your pilot." The tall, slender man gestured to the seating area that had all the markings of an elegant conference room. "Looks like you get first pick."

"Thank you." This was definitely traveling in style.

"You may keep your bag with you or stow it in the luggage closet at the rear of the passenger cabin."

She thanked him again and moved on to the seating area. Once she'd selected a seat close to a window, she dropped her handbag there and carried her overnight bag to the storage area. There was a minibar and a short corridor that led to the toilet and another door that was unmarked. She wondered if that was a private room or a store room.

"Private conference room."

Startled, she turned to face Brett Call. "Oh, thanks. I wondered about that."

Brett stashed his bags. "This is my second flight on the Colby bird." He hitched a thumb toward the bar. "Would you care for refreshments?"

Lisa shook her head. "I'm good, thanks."

Anders and Johnson had already taken their seats. Jeff Battles put his bag away and joined Brett at the bar for refreshments.

Lisa hoped it wasn't going to be this "us against them" the entire flight. In some ways, they were on opposing teams, but the operation was a joint effort. Behaving that way would be in the best interest of getting the job done.

After settling into her seat, she watched the men who represented the Equalizers. They spoke quietly as they moved through a stack of papers similar to the ones they'd viewed in Jim Colby's office. Hopefully, the two would be sharing that information with the Colby Agency representatives.

Deciding not to wait and see, Lisa spoke up as soon as Battles and Call had taken their seats. "Shall we start the briefing?"

Spencer Anders took charge. "Mr. Battles, you will be assigned to Mallory Johnson." Anders provided a photo and background info sheet on Sam's sister. "As Mrs. Colby-Camp pointed out, Mallory is a student at UCLA and you'll fit in well there."

Jeff took the photo and info sheet. "Will Miss Johnson be aware of my assignment?"

Sam shook his head. "I think it would be better if they didn't know."

Lisa was surprised at that. Was he purposely leaving his folks in the dark just so he didn't have to see them? Would he even notify them that he was in L.A.?

"Your parents are retired?" Brett inquired.

"Yes." Johnson handed photos and the needed info to Brett. "You might have a hard time keeping up with them on the golf course. Other than that, you'll find their routine fairly mundane."

"I'll maintain a command post of sorts," Anders added. "As soon as I have the location, I'll notify the team."

The *team*. That was a step in the right direction. Lisa saw an opportunity to take it one step farther. "We can use my place as the command post."

All eyes turned to her.

"The location is central, quiet and out of the high-traffic areas."

Anders nodded. "Good."

She felt Sam's gaze on her, but she avoided eye contact. "There are two phone lines, one's for a fax. My neighbors are older so they don't get out much. As long as you keep your vehicle parked in the garage there shouldn't be any questions."

"What about your partner?" This from Johnson.

Lisa's gaze met his. "He has no reason to drive by my place."

The sound system vibrated, signaling the pilot was about to make an announcement. "Ladies and gentlemen, please prepare for takeoff."

Safety belts were fastened into place across laps. Johnson was still studying her as if he suspected she'd volunteered her home for some reason that would be detrimental to him. Lisa focused her attention out the window on the people still standing near the SUVs.

Victoria Colby-Camp and her son Jim Colby waited, not quite side-by-side, since several feet separated them, for the plane to roll toward takeoff. Both watched the aircraft as if their full attention was required for proper function.

What was it between those two?

Lisa stole a glance at Sam Johnson. He'd redirected his attention to the reports spread across his lap. This uneasiness between the two of them was multifaceted for sure. There was the rage still simmering inside him at the loss of his fiancée. She sensed that emotion even as he outwardly denied it. Lisa had watched him lying in agony in that hospital room as he'd slowly recovered from the near lethal beating he'd taken that night. Before being allowed to lose consciousness, he'd been forced to watch the brutal rape and murder of the woman he loved.

Closing her eyes, Lisa shoved those images away. She'd gotten far too attached to him during those long months she and Sanford had been assigned to the case. Then the three suspects had gotten themselves murdered. Heinously so. Everyone in the division, all the way up to the chief, suspected that Sam Johnson had gotten his revenge. But there hadn't been a trace of evidence tying him to any of the scenes. Sanford had grilled him repeatedly. Followed him, harassed him, actually. Lisa had tried to pull him back, but Sanford was senior and he refused. Until the chief had ordered them off the case.

Then, three days ago, all hell broke loose. Lisa had known when The Man died that Sam Johnson's name would come up again. Somehow, Johnson had entered into an unholy alliance with the deceased leader of the Crew. His death had unleashed months of pent-up rage against Johnson. Now he was a wanted man. On more than one front. Charles Sanford would like nothing better than to nail him for multiple homicides.

When Lisa looked Sam Johnson in the eye, she

couldn't say that she was 100 percent sure that he *hadn't* killed those men, but she couldn't say he had, either. He'd had motive, that was certain. Means? She supposed so. Opportunity? Probably. But did he possess the ability to disengage emotionally so completely that he could kill not just in cold blood, but in a truly evil manner?

Lisa didn't think so.

Unfortunately, she couldn't be totally objective about that. Mainly because she'd fallen for the guy during those long months of watching him grieve. But she couldn't tell a soul, least of all him.

She felt his eyes on her once more. The woman in her pondered whether he'd ever felt that connection—that thin thread of electricity that somehow tethered them. She turned from the window, met his assessing gaze.

No matter what happened, she could never let him know how she felt. Not only would it be a mistake ethically, she was also certain it would be a huge personal error in judgment. He could never know.

If she'd been smart she would have closed the file on this case months ago. Tucked the whole package into a box and filed it away with all the other cold cases belonging to L.A. County's Priority Homicide Division.

As she held that analyzing stare, she had to admit that perhaps she wasn't nearly so smart as her detective's examination would indicate. But this had nothing to do with her intelligence level. This had to do with keeping Sam Johnson alive. If they didn't extinguish the volatile situation surrounding the murders of those three scumbags once and for all, Sam Johnson was going to pay the price:

His head delivered to the new man in charge.

Chapter Four

The Colby Agency jet touched down in the Sunshine State's Santa Monica Airfield at 5:00 p.m. Sam was the last to leave the plane. Tension rippled along his nerve endings. Irrational anxiety had clamped around his chest in a breath-halting grip. He'd sworn he would never come back here, not for anything. His family visited him in Chicago now and again, but coming back here alive was going back on the bargain he'd made.

Yet, here he was. He took the final step down onto the tarmac. Detective Lisa Smith was right, he wouldn't last long once word got out. He'd be lucky to survive this night much less the next one.

Truth was he was dead, anyway. There was no way he could hope to defuse this thing—to pretend otherwise would be a major joke on himself. If he managed to protect his family, that would have to be enough. Watts would never permit him to leave California alive. It would be a matter of pride.

Spencer Anders closed his cell phone as he approached Sam. "The rental agency dropped off the requested vehicles." He gestured to four black sedans parked near the hangar. "Keys are in the ignitions."

Anders turned to Detective Smith then. "I'd like to get set up at your place as quickly as possible."

She fished the keys from her purse and handed them to Anders. "I assume you know the location. I'll be sticking with Johnson and—" she swiveled her attention to Sam "—I doubt that's where he wants to go first."

Anders accepted the keys to her house with a nod and no argument.

Sam didn't argue her decision, either—it would be pointless. She wasn't going to let him out of her sight. As much as he hated to admit it, he was relatively certain her assistance would come in handy. He just hoped it didn't get her killed. But she was determined. He doubted anything he could say would change her mind about going with him. Why waste the effort?

"I'd like to get Call and Battles into position," Sam said to Anders. The two Colby Agency investigators were already loading their bags into two of the rentals. They understood as well as Sam did that there was no time to waste. Once word of his arrival was on the street, things could go downhill in one hell of a hurry.

"Check in with me when that's done," Anders said before heading to the third vehicle. "I don't want you out of touch for more than a couple of hours."

"Got it." Sam followed Smith to the fourth sedan.

"Would you like me to drive?" she offered.

He started to say no, but he surprised himself by saying, "Yeah."

After instructing Battles and Call to follow, Sam climbed into the passenger seat.

"I thought you might want to take in the sights," Smith commented as she drove away from the hangar.

Sam didn't respond. He'd only been gone a few months. He doubted that much had changed. Frankly, he didn't care one way or the other. He checked the side mirror to ensure Call and Battles were behind them as they merged into traffic. Anders had opted to stay on the boulevard while they took the expressway. Detective Lisa Smith lived off Santa Monica Boulevard in Century City which was pretty much a straight shot in the direction Anders chose.

Sam's folks lived a world away, in the affluent Bel-Air community. He wasn't too worried about Call being noticed hanging around in the exclusive neighborhood. Paparazzi hung around celebrity homes all the time. Not that his folks were celebrities, but there were plenty in their neighborhood.

Once in a while the local cops would advise the paparazzi to move on, but no one was ever surprised when they came right back.

"Your parents miss you."

Sam turned and stared at the detective's profile. "How would you know that?" If she had been talking to his folks...

"I call now and again to see how they're doing." She said this without looking at him.

The anger he'd kept at bay since putting life in L.A. behind him started to boil in his gut. "You have no right keeping tabs on my folks or me."

"You're wrong." She glanced at him this time. "Until this case is solved, I have every right. It's *my* case."

Sam held back the first response that rushed to the tip of his tongue. He knew this wasn't simply about clearing her record of the failure. As much as he wanted to say just that, it would be a lie. Lisa Smith was dedicated to the job. He'd known that about her long before he'd found himself a victim.

He'd worked with the L.A. County Forensics Division. For years he'd been one of the leading evidentiary experts. The techs brought in the evidence, and Sam put it all together. He'd been pivotal in solving many, many homicides. That dedication to duty had cost his fiancée her life. He'd ensured a murderer got his due, and she had paid the price.

Sam pushed the memories away. He couldn't change what had happened one night on La Cienega Boulevard nearly two years ago. It was too late to protect Anna. Way too late to make that right. But he had to protect his family. No one else needed to die because of his decisions.

"You should talk to them," Smith suggested quietly. "Let them know you're here. It's not right to keep them in the dark."

His jaw hardened against the idea that a hell of a lot wasn't right about this, but that didn't help. "The less they know the better off they are."

"Lil Watts doesn't have the same principles his uncle had. Your family's innocence in all this won't keep him from doing whatever he decides to do."

He didn't need her to tell him that. The Man, James Watts, had been a man of honor despite the fact that he'd been one of the instrumental forces in forming the Crew. Though he'd levied vengeance swiftly and fatally, he'd never once killed a man who hadn't deserved to die. The generation that came after him, including his beloved—however whacked—nephew, operated more often on impulse than honor.

Sam didn't say any more on the subject. No need to. He'd made up his mind. Nothing the detective said was going to change it. Instead, he watched as the sun dropped low in the sky, spilling its fading orange glow over the L.A. skyline in the distance. No matter what the detective said, he couldn't let sentimentality or foolish dreams get in his way.

Protecting his family was the best he could hope for. Staying alive was too much to ask.

LISA PULLED TO THE SIDE of the street directly across from the home belonging to the parents of Sam Johnson. She'd been here numerous times before. More often than Johnson needed to know, that was for sure. The house was obscured by the trees, the driveway one that wound deep into the unusually large lot before reaching the residence. The area was quiet and the surrounding homes hidden by the well-wooded landscape. This part of Bel-Air in particular was thick with trees, one of the few lushly forested neighborhoods in the L.A. area.

Call and Battles had joined Lisa and Johnson in their rental.

"Mallory should be in her evening class at this time," Battles advised. "I'll head there now unless you have additional directions."

His attention focused fully on the home where he'd grown up, Sam said, "You might want to put a tracking device on her car. Mallory can be tough to keep up with. She's had so many speeding tickets it's a miracle she hasn't lost her license already."

"I'd planned to do that," Battles acknowledged. "And perhaps one in her handbag or book bag."

"I'll relocate every few hours," Call put in, "keeping the house in my line of sight. If the neighbors on either side are on vacation I'll attempt to get closer to the property via that route."

"I'd like an update every four to six hours." Johnson shifted to face the men in the backseat. "If anything at all looks or feels wrong, I want to know it."

Call nodded. "I understand."

The two Colby Agency investigators exited the car and moved to their separate vehicles. Battles headed for the university while Call settled in on the shaded street for the evening.

"Are we ready to catch up with Anders at my place?"

Johnson pulled his attention from his parents' home and rested it on her. "First I'd like to go by the cemetery."

"It's still daylight," Lisa countered, "that's not a good idea." He'd be a sitting duck in that situation. She couldn't be sure that Watts or his people knew Johnson was back in L.A. already, but there was no need to take such an unnecessary risk.

"I can go with or without you."

She could squabble with him, maybe make him angry, but needed his cooperation. To that end, she had to go along with his request even when she didn't feel it was in his best interest.

"All right. Hillside Memorial it is then."

That he looked surprised that she had caved so easily told her that he'd expected to be able to use her resistance as an excuse to part company.

She'd made the right decision.

Hillside Memorial was in L.A; not that far, but evening traffic had gotten heavy, slowing them considerably. Convertible tops were down, music thumping, commuters were celebrating the passage of hump day. It would be all about Friday for the next twenty-four hours. That was the thing about Southern California: the weather was always perfect. One could admire the array of beautiful plants, one or the other always in bloom, and the well-kept lawns along Sunset Boulevard before the residential area gave way to the edgy clubs and restaurants. Amid such beauty it was difficult to believe that anything bad ever happened here. But that was only one side of this vibrant city.

Night would fall and other streets, those beyond the reach of all the glamour and glitz, would fill with the restless souls of those living in the depths of desperation and poverty. A vivid contrast where being a part of a gang, notorious or not, was the closest thing to belonging some people ever got.

Sam Johnson had crossed the line that separated

that life from his own. He'd found the single piece
of evidence that sent Lil Watts's older brother to
prison for murdering two cops. Lil had avenged his
brother's incarceration by ordering the execution of
Sam's fiancée. For Lisa, the story ended there. But
she needed to know what happened after that. Who
executed the three men who had carried out Lil
Watts's orders? If it was Sam, why had Lil refrained
from avenging their deaths until now? Why would
James, The Man, have kept him in check until his
death? What did James owe Sam…if anything?
Why had Sam left L.A.? The memories? Or was
that part of the deal?

Plenty of questions, not enough answers.

Hillside Memorial Park was deserted when they
arrived. The air had grown cool and crisp as the sun
slid lower into the mountains and canyons circling the
city. Lisa stayed two steps behind Johnson as he
walked through the rows of the buried along Sunset
Slope. Lisa's nerves jangled as she repeatedly surveyed the cemetery, ensuring no one was watching.

Anna Denali's headstone was black granite and
lay flush with the ground. The clean lines of her
name and dates of birth and death were all that
marred the sleek surface. No testaments to her short
life, no cameo photos. An only child, her death had
devastated her parents. They held Sam Johnson
wholly responsible for what happened. Lisa didn't

have to hear the words to know he held himself responsible, as well.

She stayed back, giving him plenty of room, as he knelt down and touched the marker that designated the woman he'd loved.

At thirty-one, Lisa was beginning to wonder if she would ever have a man feel for her what Johnson had felt for Anna Denali. Lisa had been too wedded to her job to have a decent social life. Her partner teased her nonstop that if she didn't find a man soon it would be too late to bother.

Maybe it was watching Sam Johnson agonize over losing the woman he loved that had driven the point home so completely. Lisa hadn't been completely happy with her life since. But then she hadn't been able to do anything about it since she'd been hung up on a man who was not only victim but suspect.

Such a waste of energy.

Not to mention really dumb.

Cutting herself some slack, how often did a woman spend eleven months focused so damned intently on one man? It would have been pretty hard to walk away unattached to the guy.

Her partner liked pointing out that her male counterparts didn't have that trouble. Not that she'd admitted her slip to him, but he joked about other female detectives who got involved with suspects.

In reality Lisa wasn't involved. And Sam Johnson wasn't a suspect anymore, not technically. If she could get to the truth, maybe her partner would finally let the idea that he was guilty go. Maybe Sam Johnson's life could go back to normal.

Maybe even hers would.

Watching the emotion tearing him apart as he kneeled next to his fiancée's grave wasn't exactly the fastest route to accomplishing that feat. She needed so badly to put this case behind her once and for all. As hard as she'd tried, she just couldn't get past it with all these unanswered questions haunting her.

As if he'd picked up on her thoughts, Johnson stood. "Let's go." He didn't wait for her to respond but strode back to the car.

The drive from the cemetery to her bungalow was filled with the same silence as when they'd left his parents' home. If that was the way it was going to be she would have a heck of a time learning anything at all from him. So much for cooperation. So far she'd been the only one putting forth any effort.

She parked down the block from her house. Dusk had invaded, providing some amount of cover as they hurried along the sidewalk, bags in hand. The lack of through traffic and pedestrians provided some sense of security as she scrutinized the area. There was no reason for anyone to suspect they would come here. Still, caution had to be her watchword. Sam Johnson might have a death wish, but she didn't.

"We'll enter through the back," she suggested as she cut through the narrow length of side yard that separated her house from the row of high hedges along the boundary of her neighbor's yard.

On second thought, she pulled out her cell and put in a call to Anders so he would know they were coming in. She had no desire to get shot by someone on their own team—assuming this was in fact a team effort. Their group possessed all the markings of a team, but the essential element of full collaboration was yet to be seen.

"We're at the back door now," she told Anders.

The door opened as if he'd been waiting there for her call. They hustled inside and closed out any prying eyes. The less they were seen in the open the better.

"You have several messages on your landline from your partner," Anders informed her. "I'm beginning to wonder if he really believes you're on vacation."

Lisa suppressed the initial reaction of irritation that he'd listened to her messages. "You're certain they're recent?" She was bad about erasing old messages.

"All in the last thirty-six hours. The most recent one was the only one listed as a new call. Have you been remote-accessing your machine?"

"No. I never check my messages remotely."

There was no reason for her to. Anyone she needed or wanted to hear from had her cell number. Why would Chuck do this? She dropped her bag and walked over to the answering machine to listen for herself. Four messages, all in the past thirty-six hours as Anders said, all repeating the same question: "You home yet, Smith?"

Her partner knew damned well she wasn't supposed to be home yet.

"Is it possible he has the code for accessing your machine?"

Lisa glanced at Sam, annoyed. "No. Why would he?"

Sam shrugged. "Maybe to see if you're checking your messages from here."

"He knows I hate answering machines," she argued. "The only reason I have one is because my mother complained that she could never reach me. She hates cell phones. Even then it sat in the box for months before Chuck forced me to hook it up...." He'd insisted she do it to keep her family happy.

"Did he help you do it?"

"No." Her gaze connected with Johnson's. "He set it up for me."

This was nuts. Why would he leave her messages and then check to see if she'd accessed them?

Because that would mean she was home, since she didn't know the remote access code. Why would

Chuck resort to such extreme measures to keep track of where she was on her own time?

"We'll have to leave a new message," Anders said quickly.

"Or he'll know someone has been here," Johnson added. "First we need a recording."

Anders searched the array of items he'd spread across her coffee table. "Got it." He used the palm-size machine to record as the last message Chuck Sanford had left was replayed.

This was crazy. Before she could argue, Sam was placing a call via his cell. When her machine picked up he played the recording of Sanford's voice into his cell phone. He did this only once, since there had only been one new message. The machine recorded it as if Chuck himself had just made the call.

"No answering your home phone," Johnson told her as he put his cell away. "No checking your messages."

She put up her hands. "Wait. This doesn't add up. Why would my own partner do this?"

"Because," Johnson said, as he placed his gear bag on the sofa, "he obviously doesn't believe you're on vacation. He thinks you're up to no good."

Unfortunately, her partner would be right. Lisa would be the first to admit that Chuck didn't like that she obsessed about Sam Johnson's possible inno-cence in the slaying of those three men who'd murdered his fiancée, but would he go this far to check up on her? Maybe, if he was worried about her. But that didn't make the tactic one motivated by some sinister agenda as these two obviously believed.

Still, why the hell had he learned the manufacturer-installed access code to her answering machine? Had he been banking on the idea that she wouldn't change it because she wouldn't ever use it?

What would be his motive?

Johnson planted his hands on his hips and fixed her with a look that said listen up. "Whatever you might be thinking, if we're going to be on the same team, we have to get one thing straight."

She matched his stance. "What's that?"

"Everyone is a suspect, even your beloved partner. If you really want to defuse this ticking bomb as much as you say, you're going to have to look at all involved in what happened with an eye toward assessing the possibility of their involvement. No one is exempt."

"Not even me?" If he considered her a suspect, then he needed his head examined.

"You're not the only one who can do a thorough background check, Detective," he said pointedly.

And then she knew he had learned her little secret. Even her partner didn't know about that.

"My brother's death doesn't make me a suspect," she argued, heading him off.

"Your brother died as a result of a gang shootout

in a retail store parking lot. You were twelve, your brother was fifteen. Don't pretend it didn't have an impact on your life. That's motive, Detective Smith. No matter how you look at it."

Why not put all her cards on the table? "You're right. It is motive. It's motive to become a cop. To try and stop gang killings before they happen, one at a time."

She hated the way he looked at her with his expression all full of sympathy. "This is L.A., Detective, gangs are a fact of life. So is murder. You aren't going to change that. The only thing you can hope to do is survive peaceably next to each other."

"I guess we'll just have to agree to disagree," she said resolutely. "Anna Denali was murdered by three gang members. If your version of the story is to be believed," she pointed out, "then one or more other gang members killed those three and left you looking like the perpetrator. It has to stop somewhere. Someone has to try and make a difference. Might as well be me."

The sympathy morphed instantly into fury. "I tried to make a difference, Detective," he said bitterly, "and look what it cost me."

"Are we ready to prep?" Anders asked, breaking the ensuing tense silence.

"Yeah," Johnson said, "we're ready."

His gaze never deviated from hers. It was like

he wanted her to argue with him, to prove they couldn't get through this night as a team, much less the next. But she held her tongue. If this effort didn't work, it wouldn't be on account of her stubbornness. He also stayed clear of her theory about who killed those bastards who murdered his fiancée. Maybe if she kept at him he'd admit what he knew at some point…hopefully before one or both of them were dead. Lisa pushed her frustration aside and listened up as Anders went over the gear.

Wireless communication links would keep her and Sam in touch at all times. Since Anders would be out of range, they would check in every few hours via cell phone. Tracking devices would keep him aware of their positions. The devices were small microfiber ones, which prevented detection by the naked eye. Anders would serve as the go-between for the team watching the Johnson family. That way everyone was apprised regularly and similarly.

Since Johnson insisted on a little night surveillance, Lisa changed into dark slacks and a dark pullover. L.A. nights could turn cool rapidly so she selected a lightweight blazer. She carried a black cap for tucking her hair into, but she wouldn't wear it until she needed to. She fastened her ankle holster in place and slid her .22 automatic into it. Her service revolver would be too bulky.

Sam dressed in jeans and T-shirt with an open, button-down shirt over it to hide the weapon tucked into his waistband. She didn't bother asking if he possessed a permit to carry a weapon. He'd be a fool not to carry, considering where they might end up before this night was over.

With a gear bag packed with additional rounds, flashlights, a detailed map of L.A. and surrounding communities, and Johnson's small first-aid kit, there really wasn't anything else to do. They had the cover of dark now. The only question was how he intended to make his first move.

"What's our plan?" She looked from Johnson to Anders and back. This was as far into the plan as they'd gotten on the plane.

Sam grabbed the gear bag. "Now we go put the word out."

Fear swelled in her throat. "Exactly what word is that?"

His gaze collided with hers. "That I'm back and ready to see who thinks they're big enough to fulfill that contract."

He had to be kidding. "Are you out of your mind? We won't last five minutes out there tossing your name around. We need to assess the situation. Measure the trouble waiting on the street without making our presence known."

Anders stayed out of the discussion, which told Lisa that he wasn't so hip on Johnson's plan, either.

"You can go with me and do exactly as I say or else you can stay here." Sam shrugged. "It's your call, Detective."

As she stood there too stunned to speak or act, he walked right past her headed for the back door.

"You can't possibly agree with this," she said to Anders.

"The only way to start the domino effect," Anders explained, "is to push the first one down."

"What domino effect?" Evidently these two were on some kind of wavelength she'd missed entirely.

"When you want the truth, Detective Smith, you start a chain reaction, and whoever has something to hide will always try to stop the momentum. All you and Sam have to do is start that reaction and wait and see who goes against the inertia."

She laughed, the sound was dry and wholly lacking in humor. "And stay alive in the process."

Anders acknowledged her point with a dip of his head. "That would be the most desirable scenario."

Lisa stalked off in the direction Sam had taken. Maybe if she hurried he wouldn't leave her behind. If he intended to get himself killed someone had to be there to call it in.

Assuming he didn't get her killed in the process.

Chapter Five

The Box.

Skid Row.

A human calamity. A drug supermarket where gang members from all over this city and surrounding areas came to peddle their wares—usually crack and heroin. A place where addicts and people with psychiatric disorders were found every morning sleeping on the sidewalks. The open use of drugs and five-buck tricks in the portable toilets were as common as breathing.

Sam had thought this ugly side of his hometown was something he wouldn't be facing again in this lifetime. So much for future planning.

"I hope you know what you're doing."

Sam glanced at the woman in the passenger seat. Cop or no, armed or not, anyone with half a brain would be a little nervous in this neighborhood. But this was the closest thing to a safe zone he could hope to find within the territories of violence located in and around L.A.

Rival gang members stood on the same street corners taking care of business. Everybody was just doing what they had to do to survive, and all involved respected that—the faintest glimmer of that "honor among criminals" that The Man, James Watts, had lived and died by.

Sam wondered how long any honor would last with the up-and-coming generation of gangbangers. With what he knew about Lil Watts, not long for sure.

He parked in an alley between a rundown hotel where presidents and silent-film stars once stayed— before the area was swallowed up by the evil forces of drugs and desperation and a restaurant that had closed at nine.

"Leave it parked here and it'll be gone when we come back," Smith said with a long assessing look around. Dumpsters lined the far end of the alley, the smell of grease and food refuse permeating the air. "Assuming we make it back."

"It's cool," Sam assured her. He climbed out, grabbed the bag from the backseat and locked the doors.

Sam surveyed the dark alley, lit only by one meager streetlight, taking note of the tents and the cardboard condominiums already erected and occupied for the night. By 8:00 a.m. every last one would disappear, just in time for the gates on shops to go up as they opened for business. Tourists and shoppers who visited only by the light of day would never get even the slightest hint of the nocturnal residents who camped out here every night.

Sam retrieved the bar of bath soap he'd taken from Smith's shower and marked the windows on the car to protect it from exactly what she had predicted.

"That may or may not work," she countered, obviously not inclined to put much faith in those who lived by the laws of the street.

He put the bar of soap away in the duffel and considered his handiwork. The emblem he'd used, representing a fierce South Central gang, would likely ward off any trouble. Men had been killed for grievances far more trivial than stripping a vehicle belonging to a rival gang member. He was counting on that history to make the difference.

"It's a chance we'll have to take," he said in answer to her warning. She didn't argue, but she didn't agree, either. That surprised him, but then he remembered that she was the one who needed his cooperation. She wasn't going to make any unnecessary waves.

Panhandlers with their cups outstretched lined the sidewalk beyond the alley. Sam kept his attention straight ahead. He had no desire to see the dull, listless eyes of those who had somehow managed to avoid drug addiction any more than he did the glittering ones of those verging on violent impulses by the chemicals flowing through their weakening veins.

As they entered the hotel, the once-opulent marble lobby smelled stale and musty and was in need of a cleaning. The silence and poor lighting instantly took one's senses to a higher level of alert. The clerk behind the counter looked as if he'd rather be anywhere but here. He pushed a registration card toward Sam without saying a word in welcome or instruction.

"I'd like a view of the street," Sam told him.

The clerk grunted, which Sam took as an affirmative response.

"We're getting a room?"

Sam glanced at Smith. "Yeah."

Like before, she didn't bother with any more questions. He filled out the short form, handed the clerk a bill sufficient to cover two night's room rate and accepted the keycard.

Smith didn't inquire as to his plans again until they were in the elevator headed upward.

"You're going to have to let me in on your strategy. I don't like operating in the dark."

She was annoyed at his highhandedness. Too bad. He kept his attention on the floor numbers as the slow-moving elevator idled past each. She wasn't going to walk away if he didn't play nice. He wasn't that lucky. "I don't have a plan."

Besides, he didn't have a plan, not really. Not one she would like, anyway.

She was really irritated now. But the elevator stopped and the doors slid open before she could launch what would likely be a debate or tirade. Maybe her patience couldn't keep up with her desire for his cooperation.

Sam led the way to the room, unlocked the door and waited while she went in ahead of him. He'd hesitated in a gesture of ladies first, but he doubted she cared about manners. The cop in her would want to check out the room first, would consider it her God-given right.

He'd no more than gotten the light turned on and the door closed when she lowered the boom.

"You take a room in a hotel that's a regular stop on the coroner's route and you expect me to just go along? Get real, Johnson. I need a heads-up on your strategy before this goes any further. I've been patient for about as long as I'm going to be."

Just as he'd thought. He dropped the duffel on the bed and walked over to the window. "I'm waiting for the right time. When that time comes we'll play our moves by ear." He pushed the worn drapes aside and considered the maze of seemingly innocuous streets below.

Despite her impulse to question him further, Lisa made a decision to continue cooperating. Hopefully he would do likewise when the time came. Maybe if she gained his trust, he would tell her the whole truth. As much as she hated to admit it, part of her wanted to do exactly as he'd suggested, put that old case to bed once and for all. But mainly she wanted to prove to her partner that Sam Johnson hadn't killed anyone. It was the only way he would ever really have his life back. Running away to Chicago hadn't changed anything. He had to know that.

She'd told herself a hundred times that he wasn't her problem. That she should just let the whole thing go. But the need to get this case right, to settle all the questions, wouldn't let go. This one had gotten to her. She refused to believe it was the man alone that kept haunting her.

He stayed by the window, staring out at the less-than-scenic view. The city lights far beyond the streets below offered a kinder background to the danger lurking just outside these walls. This whole situation could be handled so much easier if he would only tell her what had happened last year. His refusal to discuss any of it only made him look guilty. Add to that the fact that he didn't care what anyone thought about him one way or the other, and the result was one major roadblock.

The cell phone in her pocket vibrated, startling

her. Evidently hearing her breath catch, Johnson glanced back at her. Embarrassed at being caught on edge, she averted her gaze and focused on the call.

"Smith."

"Detective, this is Spencer Anders."

Anticipation zinged inside Lisa. "Yes, Mr. Anders." Her gaze met Johnson's as he turned to face her.

"An unmarked vehicle posted across the street from your house about forty-five minutes ago. It's not your partner, Sanford, but it's definitely a cop."

Why would the department have someone on surveillance at her place? "You're certain?"

Anders's hesitation told her he wasn't accustomed to being second-guessed. "I ran the license plate. The vehicle belongs to Los Angeles County's police department. It's listed to a Detective Hernandez."

Hernandez? What the hell? He was in Homicide. Why would he be watching her house? She doubted it would do her any good to ask Anders how he'd managed to run a plate, especially at this time of night. She didn't even want to know how he managed access to the system, period.

Pushing the irrelevant detail aside, she asked, "Your presence hasn't been detected?" If word got back to Chuck that she was working with Johnson there would be a lot of awkward tension to deal with. Technically, since she was on vacation and she wasn't breaking any laws—at least not yet—what she did was no one else's business. But this would become the whole division's business if word got out before she'd solved this case.

"I spotted him when he arrived. He has no idea I'm here."

If she were damned lucky, it would stay that way.

Then came the question she'd expected Anders to ask. "Do you know of any reason why someone from your division would be watching you?"

There was only one.

"I can only assume that Chuck suspects I'm up to something besides vacationing in Cozumel." The admission was bitter on her tongue.

"I'll keep you posted on Hernandez's movements."

Lisa thanked him and closed her phone and slid it back into her pocket. The idea that her partner didn't trust her stuck in her throat along with a host of emotions from anger to a feeling of betrayal.

"Chuck Sanford has a man hanging out in front of my house," she told Johnson.

"Are you surprised?"

That irritation he seemed to be able to rouse so easily reared its frustrating head. "What's that supposed to mean?"

"Your partner wants to pin those murders on me." Johnson shifted his attention back to the view out the window. "He knows you well enough to understand that you didn't just up and decide to take a vacation at the same time that Lil Watts is plotting to get his hands on my head. You surely realized that before you came to Chicago."

On some level maybe she had. Mostly she'd been disgusted with Chuck's attitude, but she wasn't giving Johnson the satisfaction of knowing the full extent of the tension already simmering between her and her partner of five years. Her sense of loyalty wouldn't let her charge onward without giving him the benefit of the doubt for a little while longer.

"Are you saying you didn't commit the murders?" Johnson's statement about her partner wanting to pin the murders on him seemed to indicate that mind set. But the admission would be a first. Sam Johnson had spent the last year keeping his mouth shut, sitting back and letting Homicide try its damnedest to prove him guilty…knowing, based on the glaring lack of evidence, that it wouldn't happen. If she was smart she'd walk away from this right now.

But she couldn't.

And, damn it, she hated that weakness.

"I'm not saying anything about the murders, Detective," he returned pointedly. "We're talking about you and your partner and his vendetta against me." He turned to stare out the window once more, his profile set in stone. "Have you ever considered why he wants to nail me so badly?"

Only one of the wall sconces in the rundown room

worked, but even with the poor lighting it was easy
to see the grim line of his lips. There had always been
something, some source of friction between Johnson
and Chuck. Not that her partner had ever admitted
it, but she'd picked up on it more than once.

"Charles Sanford is a twenty-five-year veteran of
LAPD's Priority Homicide Division," she argued.
"He likes solving his cases. Failing to get the bad
guy makes us all look bad. He and I just have a different opinion of who the bad guy is in this case."

"Keep telling yourself that, Detective," Johnson
said, with a sidelong glance at her, "if it makes you
sleep better at night."

He wasn't getting off that easily. She walked to
the window and stood bedside him but kept her
eyes front and center on the view beyond the
window. This close, looking him square in the eyes
wouldn't be a good idea. "How can you complain
about the way the investigation was handled when
you declined to cooperate? We had no choice but to
work around your refusal to give us the full details
we needed. Our hands were tied."

"If you'd had evidence against me, you would
have arrested me, but you didn't."

He turned his face fully toward her, those gray
eyes penetrating. The tension abruptly shifted to
something more personal with her standing so close
and looking so deeply into his eyes. The realization

that they were shoulder to shoulder with only the thin fabric of their clothes separating their skin made her heart jolt against her sternum. This close, every line and angle of his face reminded her of the nights she'd spent sitting at his bedside…waiting for him to surface from the coma those bastards had put him in.

"I keep telling myself," she said as she searched his eyes, "that your refusal to talk couldn't possibly have been about protecting anyone else. I mean, why would a guy protect the people responsible for the murder of the woman he loved and planned to marry?"

His guard went up so fast the harshness of the change took her aback, forced her to take a moment to regroup before she went on. "But it felt exactly like that was what you were doing."

He leaned toward her, as if he wanted to intimidate her, but the only thing he succeeded in doing was making her pulse skip erratically. "Things aren't always what they seem, Detective. If you looked closely enough you'd find that out."

This was the way it had been with him from the beginning. Every response was a question. Every explanation was a riddle.

"You've said that before," she countered, "and I've yet to see whatever it is you keep alluding to. Maybe this truth you believe exists only in some reality you created to camouflage what really happened."

He turned that piercing gaze back to the street below. "Then maybe you aren't really looking."

Square one. That was where they always ended up.

A muscle flexed in his jaw, belying his relaxed posture. He could be right. She studied that stony profile a moment longer. Perhaps she hadn't been looking closely enough, but she was looking now.

"What is it you're afraid of, Johnson? I know you want to protect your family, but this seems like something more. I was there during your recovery. I'm certain you're not afraid for yourself. You spent nearly a decade ferreting out the evidence to put dozens of bad guys away. What is it that scares you so badly that you'd keep the identity of a murderer a secret?"

He glared at her. "Other than for the safety of my family, I'm not afraid of anything, Detective. Don't mistake my determination to settle this in my own way for fear. This isn't about fear."

She moved her head from side to side, disgusted. "You do it every time. You say a lot, but you don't tell me anything at all."

"It's time to go." He stepped away from the window, let the shabby drapes fall back into place.

"Have you decided where we're going yet?" That he refused to keep her briefed made her want to draw her weapon and demand that he cooperate.

"It's not far." He checked his weapon. "You sure you want to do this?"

"I'm not letting you out of my sight."

Sam hated dragging her along. As much because she distracted him on some level as because of the idea that she could get herself killed following him around. The problem was neither one of those excuses was going to keep her from tagging along. He might as well make the best of her participation.

"You'd better leave your jacket behind," he warned.

She wanted to question him as to why, but she didn't. Instead she ditched the jacket that hid all those lush curves outlined so well by the black attire.

He looked away, kicked himself for noticing.

Once the door to their room closed behind them, he opted for the stairs rather than the elevator. Acquainting himself with all routes of escape could come in handy. Once he made his presence known, staying out of sight would elevate to a matter of prime importance. Every step had to be carefully calculated. It was the only way to do what had to be done without getting killed before he'd attained his goal.

Outside he took a right on the sidewalk. It was past ten now. Those who had a penchant for partying would be out en mass. The beggars and dealers were thick on the sidewalk. The smell of drugs and body odor heavy in the night air. Every imaginable means to escape reality was here for the taking if a guy had the cash. Two blocks farther there was a club, the Sahara. That was his destination.

As they neared the club, the deejay's music thumped above the boom boxes stationed on the street corners and the stereos of the cars cruising by. Cronies of Lil Watts frequently hung out at the Sahara. It was one of the few clubs where members from various gangs gathered without clashing. Sam wanted to send the scuzzball Watts a message. A few minutes in the Sahara and someone would recognize him. Word would get to Lil faster than the speed of light. As big as L.A. was, each segment of the population had its own methods and grapevines. Word of mouth was a powerful tool especially with cell phones keeping the world in touch.

The door of the club opened and the loud hip-hop spilled out behind a couple of shady-looking characters who swaggered out. Probably stringers. The runners used for going back and forth from the dealer to the mass of customers gyrating on the dance floor. Nothing like service with a personal touch.

As Sam neared the club entrance Smith stalled. "You have to be kidding."

He reached for patience, didn't find it. "Listen, if you can't handle this situation, then maybe you should go back to the room. This is the way it has to happen. *This* is my plan."

"You really do have a death wish, Johnson."

He considered her a moment, but decided not to debate her assertion. There had been a time in all this when he had been teetering on that edge, just wishing someone would give him the right push. But no more. He had a new life in Chicago and he wanted this done so he could get back to it. If Smith was nervous about his plan, she should say so now. Once they got inside, any second thoughts would be too late.

"The question is—" he draped his arm around her shoulders, felt her tense "—do you really want the truth badly enough to do whatever is necessary to get it?"

Well, he had her there. Lisa didn't answer, he knew what she wanted. She let him guide her into the club as if they were a couple out on the town. He paid the cover charge and merged into the crowd. The crush of bodies and the deafening throb of music fragmented her thoughts. The suspicious looks cast in their direction didn't slow Johnson's plunge through the throng. The weapon in her ankle holster felt a world away. She'd been in spots like this before, but always with her badge visible and her weapon more accessible in her shoulder holster. Going in like this she felt naked and vulnerable.

Johnson located a vacant spot at the bar and claimed it. He kept his arm around her shoulders and her body drawn close to his. That part was for show. Her foolish heart didn't appear to know the difference since it pounded unreasonably. Now wasn't a good time to silently rail at herself for being hung up on the guy, but later, when she wasn't compacted amid a couple hundred dope heads she would give herself hell for allowing the reaction.

The bartender, whose physical description fit the bill of big, bad and one-smart-remark-away-from-going-ballistic, paused to get their drink order, though didn't bother asking what they would have. Instead he waited, pulling off the whole silent and brooding act to the max.

Johnson looked at her. "Beer?"

She nodded. Why not? She wasn't technically on duty.

"Two beers," he said, holding up two fingers and then pointing at the bottled brew in the hand of the nearest patron so he wouldn't have to shout against the blare of music.

Lisa resisted the impulse to take stock of the club. It was instinct to evaluate her position in any given situation, but that would only reveal the fact that she didn't belong here. Not an optimal scenario by any stretch of the imagination.

Johnson leaned his head close to hers. "You see those two guys at the other end of the bar?"

She glanced that way without turning her head. "Yeah." Two skinny guys who looked as if they had recently escaped rehab.

"One of them used to work for Lil Watts. I don't know about now, but you can rest assured that any opportunity to gain brownie points would be pounced upon."

This was precisely what she had feared he had in mind.

She lifted her lips to his ear so she could keep her voice down as low as possible. "I don't think this is a good idea, Sam." She used his first name to really get his attention and because her heart was thundering in her chest and messing with her ability to think straight. She could see this ending badly far too rapidly. Just being here was dangerous enough without calling unnecessary attention their way.

He turned his face to hers, so close she could feel his breath on her lips. He dodged her mouth barely and rested his lips fully against her hair to whisper directly in her ear. "I know what I'm doing. You're going to have to trust me, Smith. Can you do that?"

For several tension-filled beats she couldn't decide how to respond. Maybe it was the distraction of his jaw pressed against her cheek, or his lips lingering close to her sensitive lobe…but she couldn't think nearly quickly enough to react appropriately.

She'd made up her mind that she was going to see this through when she went to the Colby Agency. Backing out now would be a mistake. She needed to know the truth. And whether he would ever admit it or not, he needed it, too, for more reasons than just protecting his family. Instinct nudged at her, warning that he was as much in the dark on some level as she was. But she needed to be able to prove that…to prove what really happened. There had already been way too much speculation.

The only way they were going to get this done was to do it together.

She lifted her chin, accidentally brushed her lips against the lobe of his ear when she'd meant to stop just short of doing that. She felt him tense. So, she wasn't the only one feeling the vibes of this nonsensical attraction.

"I can do that…for a little while."

The plop of bottles against the counter drew her attention to the bartender who waited for payment. This wasn't the sort of establishment where a patron could run a tab.

Sam tossed a couple of bills on the counter before handing one of the sweating bottles to her. He picked up the other and downed a swallow. She got a little lost in watching the movement of his lips, his throat and his fingers on the bottle. Taking a drink of the cold brew, she reminded herself of something very, very important. She couldn't be 100 percent certain that the man standing so close wasn't a brutal killer.

But she would take her chances and trust him.

She told herself it had nothing to do with all those long nights she'd watched him lying there so close to death, but the truth was she couldn't be sure about that, either.

Whatever the case, it was way too late to change her mind now.

Johnson was suddenly wrenched away from her. She pivoted in time to see a big guy go nose to nose with him.

"I know you," the huge man growled.

"Well, then," Johnson said far more calmly than he had a right to, "you have me at a disadvantage, because I don't know you."

Before Lisa could go for her weapon considering she was hemmed against the bar by the two men, Johnson had whipped out his 9 mm with his free hand and shoved it into the underside of the big guy's fleshy chin. The atmosphere around them changed instantly…anyone standing close by went on alert, fully prepared to kill or be killed if necessary.

"But I'm willing to get to know you a whole lot better if you're interested," Johnson offered.

Four more men crowded in around them. Lisa's fingers itched to go for her weapon or her phone, but she knew better than to make any sudden moves. Not with these guys looking all too ready for a shoot-out.

"Nah," the big guy with the barrel of Johnson's weapon jabbed in his throat said, "I don't see no point in wasting my time getting to know a dead man."

He let go of Johnson's arm and Johnson lowered his weapon.

The big guy glanced at his buddies. "Let's go. This place's too crowded."

When the men had moved away, Lisa put a hand on Johnson's sleeve. "We should get out of here."

Sam picked up his beer. "Finish your drink. There's plenty of time."

She tried to be as calm as he was, but that wasn't happening. Had Johnson forgotten how quickly even a cop, especially one without backup, could get dead in a joint like this? The best training taught a cop when to use her common sense. *This* was bad. The beer tasted bitter on her tongue…and every eye in the club felt as if it was cutting through her back like a bullet.

They would be damned lucky to get out of here alive.

Chapter Six

Jim Colby's cell phone vibrated on the bedside table. He reached for it and Tasha snuggled closer to him. Ignoring the call crossed his mind. This was the first night he'd gotten home at a decent hour in days. He'd like it to carry through the whole night. But a call coming at this time of night was generally not good news. He peered at the display to identify the caller before answering. He hated to risk waking up his wife, but depending upon the caller…

Victoria.

No way could he ignore a call from his mother. He pressed the talk button. "Yeah."

"Jim, there's been a development."

"Just a minute."

As much as he hated to, Jim slipped out of the bed

and pulled the covers up around his still sleeping wife. He eased out of the bedroom and closed the door.

"What kind of development?" As he waited for his mother's response he walked quietly down the hall and peeked into his baby girl's room. She slept like an angel. He moved on to the staircase and started downward as he refocused his attention on the call.

"The Johnson family had to be briefed on the situation."

Jim stilled on the bottom step. "What do you mean 'briefed'?" He tamped down the suspicion and irritation that instantly twisted in his gut.

"Mallory confronted Jeff. I'm afraid there was no choice."

Jim's fingers tightened on the banister. "So you're telling me that your man Battles couldn't find a way to prevent blowing his cover?" It wasn't like a Colby Agency investigator to fall down on the job like that.

"I'm afraid it wasn't as simple as that. I made the final decision. Jeff felt the distance he was forced to maintain while keeping up with her schedule put Mallory in unnecessary jeopardy. In addition, there was a fiancé who complicated matters."

"Did you speak with Sam first?" Jim braced for the answer he already knew even before he asked.

"There was no time. Spencer indicated that Sam and Lisa were unreachable."

Jim forked his fingers through his hair. "You should have called me first." This situation between him and his mother had gotten entirely out of hand. Victoria couldn't seem to come to terms with his ability to take care of business. At first he hadn't minded, but things were different now. He was fully capable of making decisions. He didn't need her making them for him.

"Our people are working together as a team. I don't see the problem, Jim. Tasha told me this was the first night you'd been home in time for dinner all week. I didn't want to disturb your family time. I almost didn't call tonight at all, but evidently Mr. Johnson is refusing to cooperate and insists that Sam call him."

Great. Just great. Jim held his temper in check, as hard as that proved. "You're aware that Sam didn't want his family to be burdened with his presence in L.A."

"Yes, but I believe that was a shortsighted decision."

Enough. "Victoria, I appreciate that you're accustomed to running the Colby Agency as you see fit. But this is not solely a Colby Agency operation. Any deviations in strategy on this case should be run by me before being implemented. I thought we had an understanding."

"Jim, this shouldn't be about egos or who's in

charge. Lives are at stake here. There is no time for conference calls. I've been doing this for a very long time. My investigators are highly trained in providing personal security. I'm not so sure Sam understood the ramifications of his request to keep his family in the dark."

She simply didn't get it. It was all black-and-white and by the rules for her. Jim had learned first-hand that life didn't always follow the rules and there was far more gray than there was black-and-white.

"I can't change a decision that's already been enacted," he allowed as he strode into the kitchen for a drink. He was going to be up for a while. Damage control would be necessary. Sam was not going to like having his decisions reversed. Jim opened the fridge and reached for a bottle of water. "But this can't happen again, Victoria." He twisted off the top and downed a swallow while he waited for her reaction.

"I take it you don't agree with my decision."

Maybe he'd been too subtle. "This is primarily my operation. Sam and I make the rules. From this moment forward unless there is clear and present danger no changes are implemented without running them by one of us first."

Silence.

"That mindset is unreasonable, Jim. I appreciate your prospective, as well as Sam's, but I can't go along with a flawed strategy."

Jim set his bottle on the counter. This was the moment that had been coming for a long while now. If he just let it go, Victoria would never understand that she was stifling him.

"I'm not sure we should have this conversation over the phone."

More of that thick silence.

"This isn't a contest about who needs to be in charge, Jim. This is about making the right decisions. Are you questioning my ability to do so?"

"Evidently, you're questioning mine." He shook his head slowly, reached for the sweating bottle.

"I'm not questioning you, Jim, I'm simply looking out for all involved with this operation from a vantage point of nearly three decades of investigative and security work. I don't understand why you can't see that. You should trust my instincts."

"The way you trust mine," he suggested.

The hesitation before she responded was answer enough. She still saw him as that screwed-up guy who'd operated with only one focus: kill anything that got in his way. He'd changed. She, of all people, should have recognized that by now.

"I'm sorry, Jim, I can't make bad calls because I'm afraid of hurting your feelings. This is a business that requires swift, decisive action. There isn't always time to operate under strict protocols."

That was clear enough.

"You're right. From now on, I'll give the orders. If your people have a problem with that, I'll replace them with my people. Is that understood?"

"I don't think we need to go down that road, Jim."

He hated to do this, but she had to understand that this overprotective mentality had to cease. There appeared to be no other way to make her see that she was seriously stepping on his toes.

"I'm afraid we're already on that road, Victoria. Now, if there are no other questions, I need to do some damage control."

He didn't wait for her argument or even a response. He pushed the End Call button. For several minutes he stared at the phone. He'd just hung up on his mother. How the hell had they reached this point? It was as if she had slowly but surely come to distrust his every decision and deed. She'd been so supportive when he'd decided to go out on his own. Was this her way of letting him know how much that decision had hurt her?

The last thing in this world he wanted to do was hurt his mother…and yet there appeared to be no other way to get the point across.

Victoria Colby-Camp was not a woman easily swayed from her beliefs. If they didn't find neutral ground soon, he wasn't sure where their relationship was going to end up.

Chapter Seven

Sahara Club
Los Angeles

Sam placed his empty bottle on the counter. The bartender glanced in his direction, but Sam didn't give him any indication of needing a second round.

He pulled Smith closer. "Time to go."

Pushing his way through the crowd, he kept that arm tight around her. Though he knew she was armed and perfectly capable of taking care of herself, he suddenly felt solely responsible for her safety. If she got hurt in this place he'd have no one to blame but himself. No matter that the decision to come along had been hers, this was his problem.

He didn't breathe easily until they had cleared the door. Traffic had picked up on the street. The crowd had drifted into cliques on the sidewalks. The blocks between them and where he'd left the rental felt like a mile with every face they passed scrutinizing him. Or maybe he was only being paranoid. If word hadn't reached Lil Watts already it wouldn't be long. Getting off the street before that happened was imperative. Every move had to be timed perfectly for his plan to work.

Lisa pulled away from him as they turned into the alley. She moved around to the passenger side of the rental as he headed for the driver's door.

"Where to now?" she asked, clearly frustrated.

"I been protecting your interests, bro."

Sam's gaze shot across the top of the car. A young man stepped out of the shadows and toward Smith. He flashed the knife in his hand at her when she would have made a defensive maneuver. The man moved up behind her, wrapped his left arm around her waist to hold her and positioned the knife in a way that clarified his intent. His clothes were street rags, his face and arms grungy.

"I appreciate that. What do I owe you, *bro?*" Sam asked as he sent a reassuring glance at Smith. She didn't look scared, mostly she looked ticked off.

"I figure my expert skill's worth at least one dead president," he puffed out, feeling cocky now. "Old Ben Franklin might do the trick."

"I've got you covered." Sam ordered his heart to slow as he reached one millimeter at a time for some cash.

"Make sure that's your wallet you're going for, my friend." The jerk pressed the knife to Smith's cheek. "I'd sure hate to mess up her pretty face."

Sam pulled a one-hundred-dollar bill from his pocket.

The guy's eyes lit up. "That's what I'm talking about."

In that split second when he relaxed his guard, his full attention on the money, Smith pulled a move on him. An elbow into his gut with just the right amount of twist from her upper body sent him stumbling over her left leg which she shot out behind her as she made that turn. The momentum put the man on the ground.

By the time Sam rounded the hood Smith had drawn her handgun and had it pressed against the center of his forehead. "Why don't we call it your good deed for this lifetime?" she suggested.

"Whatever you say, lady," he urged, his eyes as round as Frisbees.

The knife lay on the ground just out of reach. Sam picked it up and looked it over before flashing it at Smith. "Too bad. Only six inches."

She backed off. "Next time," she warned, "you'd better have more than that when you come after me."

The guy scrambled up and ran like hell.

"I could've paid the guy," Sam said with a smile he couldn't seem to rein in.

"Get in the car, Johnson, before he comes back with his friends."

Before sliding behind the wheel, he retrieved a small towel from the duffel and cleaned the soaped symbols off the windows. He tossed the towel into the back and settled into the driver's seat.

"That towel's part of a matching set," she said as he started the engine.

"Don't worry." He backed out of the alley, careful of the pedestrians on the sidewalk. When he'd hit the street and shifted into Drive, he added, "I'll have it dry-cleaned."

"Where are we going now?" Lisa had presumed they would go back to the hotel. Since he hadn't opted to tell her any more details of his plan, she had no idea what came next. She'd tried to keep an open mind, but his determination to close her out was becoming tedious.

"I don't know about you," he braked for a light, "but I'm starved. I thought I'd find a drive-through. Burgers sound okay to you?"

"As long as they have fries." She could definitely eat. Lunch had been a long time ago.

The buzz of a cell phone interrupted the silence that ensued. Johnson removed the phone from his pocket. She told herself not to watch his every move with an avid interest that had nothing to do with solving the case, but the order went ignored.

"Johnson."

The way his lips compressed told her this wasn't news he'd wanted to hear.

"Yeah. I'm on my way now."

When he'd put the phone away she waited another full minute or so before she asked, "Trouble?" It would have made life so much simpler if he just chose to keep her informed.

"We have to make a midnight house call."

Another minute passed, and he still didn't say to where or to whom. "How many guesses do I get?" This was bordering on ridiculous. She could not operate in the dark!

"I have a command performance. My parents found out I'm here."

She hadn't agreed with him keeping his presence a secret from his family, but having them suddenly discover the truth didn't feel right. "How did they find out?"

His gaze steady on the street. "That part's not clear. However it happened, Jim Colby is not a happy man."

Considering Victoria's people were on security detail with Johnson's family, it only made sense that the leak had something to do with Battles or Call. If that were the case, Jim Colby's unhappiness would be with his mother. Lisa sensed the explosion coming ever nearer. She wasn't sure those two understood that they were about to cross a line of no return.

Lisa hoped for their sakes that mother and son got this thing worked out before it went that far.

Without the commuter traffic jams of the daylight hours, the drive to Bel-Air was accomplished in record time. Lisa had lived here her entire life and the transition from gaudy neon on the Strip to elegant architecture on the Bel-Air end of Sunset Boulevard still amazed her.

Both rentals belonging to the Colby Agency investigators were in the driveway of the Johnson home.

"Do you want me to go in?" she asked when he'd parked.

Sam stared at the house for a few moments where he'd grown up before he responded. "Everyone else is in there, you might as well join the crowd."

Lisa emerged from the car and followed him to the front door. He reached for the bell, but the door opened before he could press it. An older version of Sam stood in the open doorway.

"You have some explaining to do."

No hello, no hug. His father was angry. Lisa felt uncomfortable being caught in the middle of this family business.

Inside, beyond the entry hall, Call and Battles waited in the luxurious living room. Lisa stayed there while Sam followed his father deeper into the house. She surveyed the room, admired the opulence during the awkward moment that followed.

"Nice place," Brett Call noted when their gazes bumped.

"Yeah." Lisa sat down on the sofa next to him. "What happened?" she asked Battles who still stood. Too restless to sit, she surmised.

"Sam apparently didn't know his sister has a fiancé." Battles rubbed the back of his neck. "Suffice it to say the guy had a problem with how I was watching his girlfriend."

It would have helped if they had been more fully informed as to the status of the various family members. "Don't feel bad," she said, mostly to make Battles feel better, "I'm pretty much operating in the dark. Following after Johnson like a lost puppy." It definitely felt exactly like that. She had no choice but to react rather than act, never a good scenario.

"So, Victoria gave you two the go-ahead to brief the family?" Without her son's permission. That part was easy to guess.

Call nodded. "It was the only solution." He glanced in the direction Johnson had disappeared with his father. "I'm certain Mr. Colby wasn't any more thrilled to hear about her decision than Mr. Johnson."

"I checked in with Spencer Anders," Call said, "to get word to you and Mr. Johnson, but he indicated that the two of you were unreachable and didn't seem inclined to interrupt."

To some degree she and Johnson *had* been unreachable. Still, sending a text message to either her phone or to Johnson's might have alleviated this tense reunion. At the very least the attempt might have satisfied Jim Colby.

"I'll ask Johnson to speak to Anders about the lapse in communications." She looked from Battles to Call. "We need this team working together."

Call nodded. "The results could be disastrous if we keep working around each other like this."

That was the problem. Sam Johnson had kept the whole world in the dark for the past year. She wasn't sure there was anything she could do or say that would change that.

And Call was right, the end result could be disastrous.

SAM'S ENTIRE FAMILY had been waiting for him in the den. His explanation of what he was doing here and just how much danger they were in didn't have the effect he'd hoped for. All three merely stared at him after his informative monologue.

"You expect us to live in fear?" This from his father.

"I have a life," Mallory said pointedly. "I have classes and a job. And," she emphasized, "a fiancé. It would have been nice to know about this, rather than learn what was going on by happenstance."

His mother waited until last to speak. "Are you

telling us that the leader of this gang wants you dead?" she asked.

Straight to the heart of the matter. "Yes." No use lying now. "I knew he would use one or all of you to get to me if I didn't come and face the music… so to speak."

"Why didn't Lisa tell us about this?" Samuel Johnson, Sr., demanded.

Lisa, not Detective Smith. Well, well, the detective had been busy since Sam's departure. She'd managed to get on a first-name basis with his father. That was a major coup.

"Because the only way I would allow her to be involved was if she did so on my terms."

"Son," his mother wrung her hands together, "why aren't you letting the police handle this? This is far too dangerous for you to try and do alone. These people won't hesitate to kill you to protect their secrets. The police have an obligation to protect you. Why don't you let them do their job?"

Mallory jumped up from her seat and started to pace. "Good grief, Mother, surely you know he can't go to the police. They think he's the one who murdered those three gangbangers. They'd like nothing better than to have him rotting away in jail. I think Lisa is the only one who believes he's innocent."

Well said. He'd always been able to count on his younger sister to stand up for him. There wasn't a single instance of her support in the past that he appreciated more than now. He was counting on her to help him persuade their parents to cooperate with their security detail.

"Well, perhaps," Samuel offered, "if he would cooperate with the detectives, they would be a bit more open-minded."

He and his father disagreed on that one, but he wasn't going there tonight.

"Detective Smith and I are going to get this straightened out." Sam was definitely appreciative of her participation just now. "But I need your full cooperation with your security detail. I can't protect you from this if you refuse to work with me."

He held his breath, prayed like hell they would go along. He didn't know what he would do if they refused to. Endangering their lives was the last thing he wanted to do.

"And if we don't?" his mother countered. She would much prefer he just turn all this over to the police and hope they would get the job done. But she was living in a fantasy world where scumbags like Lil Watts didn't exist. "Will you go to the police, then?"

So naive. But she was his mother and he loved her.

"If you refuse to cooperate, then I'll have no choice but to do what I have to do to protect you."

"Meaning?" Mallory prodded, her arms crossed protectively over her chest.

"I'll turn myself over to the gang leader who wants my head."

His mother's face paled, and Mallory's turned a brilliant crimson with fury.

"Was that really necessary?" his father groused. "Sam, you must know that we're worried sick about you as it is. You ran off to Chicago with hardly a goodbye or go-to-hell to us. What're we supposed to think?"

Sam took a breath. Hated himself for doing this to his family. But keeping them safe was far more important than sparing their feelings. "I'm trying my best to get on with my life. But this is beyond my control. You can either help me get through it or you can force my hand." He looked from one to the other, ending with Mallory. "What's it going to be?"

He could see in her eyes that Mallory wanted to demand more answers, but thankfully she appeared to see the desperation in his. "I'll do whatever you need me to do, Sammy."

He relaxed marginally. "Thanks, sis." He couldn't remember the last time she'd called him that or vice versa. It felt good.

Samuel Johnson cleared his throat. "Well, if it'll help you get through this, then we'll do what we have to do, as well." He stepped forward, putting himself within arm's reach. "Don't we always?" Then he pulled his son into a bear hug. "Just don't get yourself killed."

Sam held on for longer than he meant to, but he just couldn't help himself. Then he hugged his mother, who cried, and then Mallory, who cursed him softly, but he knew she didn't mean a word of it.

"When this is done," his sister whispered in his ear before pulling away, "I'm going to kick your ass for putting us through this."

He hugged her tighter. "And I'll gladly let you."

When the Johnsons had composed themselves, Sam called the others in and they ran through a quick briefing to make sure everyone was on the same page. As much as he loved his family, he was glad to get out of there.

He couldn't bear being in their presence with the knowledge hounding him that his being there could get them killed.

"Where to now?" Lisa asked as Johnson turned the car around. He'd given an impressive pep talk in there about cooperation and team work. Funny, all that enthusiasm appeared to vanish into thin air as soon as they walked out the door.

"Back to the hotel."

She should have guessed. "You know there are people who likely saw us come out of there earlier tonight. That's one of the first places Watts will look when he gets the word."

Johnson pulled out onto the street. "That's what I'm counting on."

She'd been right all along. He did have a death wish.

"SLEEP IF YOU NEED TO."

He stared at the window as he made this statement. That was where he'd stationed himself as soon as they'd arrived back at the hotel.

"Fine." One of them had to get some sleep.

She took off her sneakers and socks, put her ankle holster in the drawer of the bedside table and her .22 under her pillow. After folding down the worn-out comforter, she lay back on the cool sheets. They looked clean enough. She was fairly certain the less-than-pleasant odor in the room was the carpet. She closed her eyes. Johnson had already turned out the dim sconce, leaving the room dark but for the light coming in through the window.

Sleep really would be a good thing. Even though she'd gotten into a reclining position and closed her eyes, her brain wouldn't shut down. She kept seeing images of shoot-outs and the shiny steel blades of knives.

"You know they're going to kill you, don't you?" she heard herself ask.

Had he really considered the reality that they were trapped in this fleabag hotel? A flimsy locked door wasn't going to protect them from anyone who really wanted in.

"They're going to try."

The deep, gravelly sound of his voice made her restless. She refused to open her eyes. Looking at him would only make it worse, make her feel those things she wasn't supposed to feel. Dumb, Lisa. Really dumb.

"It would be so easy to get you the kind of backup you need if you'd only tell me the whole story, Sam." She did open her eyes then. Why did he refuse to tell her the truth? He was an expert in finding evidence when all others would give up, he surely understood how important the truth was in any scenario. Everything looked different when the real story was told. No matter how guilty he appeared, coming clean could make all the difference. She'd been telling herself for a year now that what he was hiding couldn't possibly be anything that would incriminate him. She just couldn't believe he would have killed those men that way.

Gutted like fish. What kind of person ripped a man's intestines out of his body with him still breathing?

Not this one.

She was certain.

He turned away from the window. The drapes fell back into place behind him. "Do you really want to know the truth? You talk about it like it's some sort of drug that will give you the rush you've waited for your whole life." He took a step toward the bed. "But are you sure you *really* want to know?"

Lisa scooted up to a sitting position as he took a second step. "I asked, didn't I?"

"The incision was as clean as if a surgeon had set a scalpel to the flesh," he said as he sat down on the edge of the mattress, forcing her to move over to accommodate him.

"I read the autopsy report," she reminded him.

Johnson looked directly at her, his gray eyes distant as if he were remembering the images rather than recalling the autopsy report. "The first man suffered a heart attack before he'd even bled out. But the last two, they were younger, stronger, they felt every second of the pain until there was no longer enough blood in their vessels to keep their heart pumping. And they couldn't do a thing to help themselves because their hands and feet were tied. They were helpless. Just like she was." The distance disappeared and rage blazed, turning those gray eyes to liquid steel. "They tied her up just like that and then took turns having her. When they'd finished they gutted her. I remember every second of every minute she lived until her heart finally stopped."

For the first time since she and her partner had found the first of those three victims, she had to ask herself if she'd been wrong. Could Sam Johnson have killed those three lowlifes?

One corner of his mouth twitched with the beginnings of a smile. "Makes you wonder, doesn't it?"

She shoved at his chest. "You bastard. That's what you want me to do."

The door flew open and banged against the wall. A dozen men poured into the room.

Lisa was on her feet with her weapon leveled before the first one reached the bed.

"Don't move," she ordered the one nearest her position.

The sound of rounds being racked in half a dozen weapons jerked her attention to the business ends of the guns, all aimed directly at her head.

"Lower your weapon, Smith," Johnson said. "This is one of those no-win situations they talked about at the police academy."

Knowing he was right, but hating like hell to admit it, she lowered her weapon. Before she'd slid her finger away from the trigger, the .22 was snatched out of her hand. Johnson's 9 mm was taken, too.

"You have an appointment." The man who appeared to be in charge informed Johnson with nothing more than a condescending look in Lisa's direction.

Johnson flared his palms. "I'm all yours."

Lisa hoped like hell he was so calm because he knew something she didn't.

Something that meant they weren't going to die.

Chapter Eight

The streets looked empty as they drove through the Southside community. Not surprising. People didn't come out at night for fear of ending up as some form of collateral damage. At night these streets were owned by the guardians who protected their turf at all costs.

Sam glanced back at Smith. The guy in the red bandanna on her left held an AK-47 while the one on her right, directly behind Sam, preferred a .40 caliber handgun. The twenty-year-old Chevy was pimped-out to the max, complete with bulletproof glass, as was the SUV leading the four-vehicle convoy.

As they neared their destination, sentries stood on the corners, putting through calls on their cell phones to signal that the convoy was arriving. The small single-family bungalows on either side of the street gave way to high-rise apartment buildings with their graffiti-covered, bullet-pocked walls.

Farther down the street, the lights of a church stood out like a hopeful beacon in the night…just a little too far away to be of any use.

Sam wasn't worried about dying tonight, not from these guys, anyway. Their red bandannas and the tattoos they bore marked them as Nation, not Crew. Lil Watts was the latter. Whoever had requested his company tonight had nothing to do with the threat to his life.

Unless, of course, there was a price on his head that could settle some score that needed to be resolved between the two infamous gangs. No way to know for sure. Sam's only choice was to wait and see. He hadn't expected this reaction to come first, but as long as the reactions were occurring he had to consider his endeavor so far to be successful. He doubted that Smith saw it that way, but she was looking from a cop's perspective. During the past year, Sam had learned to put all he thought he knew aside. This world had its own rules. Recognizing and respecting those rules was a huge step in the direction of survival.

The scattering of duplexes beyond the high-rises were rigged for battle. Bars on the windows and guards stationed at every door. Headquarters, Sam presumed. This block would be their destination.

Once the SUV had pulled into the short driveway of one bungalow, the Chevy halted at the curb.

Doors opened and drivers and passengers unloaded. The guy with the .40 cal prodded Sam toward the house while the AK-47-toting thug hustled Smith in that direction.

Inside they were taken to an empty room and abandoned.

"Maybe you've forgotten your geography," Smith commented as she took in the twelve-by-twelve prison, "but this is not good. There are no homicides in this neighborhood. No drug dealing, no turf fighting. Nothing. This is where the trials are carried out—the decisions on who will live and who will die."

Sam tried to make light of the situation. "Well, at least we don't have to worry about dying here."

She walked over to the boarded-up window. "That's for sure. They'll take us someplace else to do that. This is the neighborhood Buster Houston calls home." She turned to Sam and waited expectantly as if she anticipated some particular reaction to the name.

He knew who Buster Houston was. Who didn't? A legend. One of the founding members of the Nation. Well into seventy, he preached peace and tolerance like a TV evangelist, despite the fact those around him were armed to the teeth.

"I'm curious to see what Mr. Houston has to say," Sam said, which clearly wasn't what she'd wanted to hear.

"Think about it, Sam," she said, using his first name again. He didn't know why that bothered him, but it did. "There's an agenda. This man doesn't waste his time. He wants something from us. That can't be good."

"Maybe."

She was right in that Houston wouldn't waste his time. But whatever he wanted wasn't necessarily bad for Sam's agenda. This could actually work to his advantage, so long as Smith's presence didn't create any unnecessary friction. The only cops found in this territory were dead ones.

The door opened and four men entered and took up positions around the room, each armed with serious fire power. Then Buster Houston walked in. Dressed completely in black, fedora included, his presence overwhelmed the room. Anyone even remotely versed in gangland history knew what a pivotal role this man had played. Despite his age he still radiated an air of danger.

"Sam Johnson," he said as he clasped his hands behind him, "your return surprises me."

Sam braced for retaliation. "Then you're obviously not in tune with the news on the street."

Houston shook his head, signaling his henchmen not to respond physically to the verbal disrespect. "What news would that be?" he asked Sam as if he had no idea what he meant.

"Watts wants my head. Surely you've heard about the edict he issued. Apparently my deal with his uncle is no good after his death."

Houston glanced at the guard standing closest to Smith. "What I have to say to that is between the two of us. I don't speak freely in front of anyone who carries a badge."

Lisa tensed. The impact of Houston's words hit her at the same time the man standing right behind her grabbed her arm and pushed her toward the door.

"Johnson," she urged, glancing back at him. Why didn't he tell this guy to allow her to stay?

When he didn't look at her or speak up, she knew that he didn't want her privy to the conversation.

So much for teamwork.

She was ushered into the hall and toward what had once been a kitchen but which now served as a waylay station for Houston's thugs.

Five men waited there. All looked dangerous, but she'd seen worse. Since the guard assigned to her didn't offer to restrain her, she relaxed against the counter and waited. Whatever Johnson and Houston had to talk about, she doubted it would take long. Most of these guys were men of few words. The idea that she and Johnson had gotten this far, unmasked and with their hearts still beating, was a major coup. Like Watts, Houston's home base moved so often that even the Gang Division of LAPD couldn't keep up with his location. This place would be abandoned by daylight.

That's why Houston wasn't worried about what she saw. Still, this was definitely an unusual encounter.

"I know you."

Her attention flew to the larger of the two men loitering near the refrigerator. He stepped forward, his eyes slitted with accusation. Déjà vu. Hadn't she and Johnson just gone through this in the club?

"You and your partner framed my cousin Sean Hastings," the gangbanger pronounced as if passing sentence.

His cohorts went on the alert, dark eyes glaring at her with that same accusation, while the man who'd spoken stepped into her personal space.

"He didn't kill nobody and he got fifteen." He sneered down at her. "You needed a suspect and you nailed an innocent man."

Lisa vaguely remembered the Hastings case. Last year. Shot his dealer for roughing him up. The kid had the murder weapon in his possession and he had no alibi. Her partner got a confession out of him. Lisa hadn't approved of his methods, but there were times when nothing else would get the job done, according to most veterans she knew on the force.

She should have kept her mouth shut. But the six

feet of angry hoodlum glaring down at her made the feat impossible.

"Sean confessed. He had the murder weapon in his possession. The case was cut-and-dried."

He laughed, as did everyone in the room. "Things are always cut-and-dried when a cop wants to close a case. Nobody cared, just another dealer shot dead and off the streets. Didn't make no difference who you nailed for doing the deed. An investment in the future, two for the price of one."

She couldn't deny his final charge. Any cop would be all the more pleased if a suspect with a long rap sheet got his due in a big way. One case, one trial, two criminals off the street. Made everyone, including the D.A., happy.

"That confession was bull," the guy said bitterly. "Maybe you don't know your partner as well as you think you do. Or maybe—" he leaned his face closer to hers "—you're just as bad as he is."

Lisa felt a spike of fear. If this guy got his buddies riled up, there could be trouble, whether the boss in the other room wanted it or not. She had two choices, she could stay cool and see how this played out or she could call this hothead's bluff.

"Maybe your cousin didn't tell you the whole story," she said, meeting that menacing glare head-on.

A muscle jumped in his tense jaw. "And maybe your partner is keeping you in the dark about the way things really work when a 187 goes down in certain neighborhoods. You should ask him sometime."

Lisa held his glower, schooling any reaction to his mention of the penal code for murder. "Maybe I will."

"Let's go," a voice called from the hall.

The guy glaring down at her backed off, and Lisa took her first deep breath since he'd spoken.

She pushed off from the counter, one of her five guards coming up behind her to ensure she moved forward. Johnson and Buster Houston waited in what had once been a living room. Since Johnson appeared to be in one piece, she assumed the conversation had been civil. As long as Johnson gave her a blow-by-blow accounting of what went on in that room she would overlook the fact that he hadn't insisted she be allowed to stay.

Houston said to one of his men. "Leave them the way you found them."

Lisa felt the tension in her muscles release fractionally. She doubted any of these men, who were closest to the leader, would dare cross him. Which meant she and Johnson might just live to argue about the way he'd handled this little consultation.

Johnson still hadn't said a word as they were loaded into the Chevy and headed back across town. Since he sat in the front seat with the driver, she couldn't exactly interrogate him. She couldn't even make eye contact unless he chose to do so. The guy who'd questioned her regarding his cousin sat in the backseat with her along with one of his pals. She kept her attention straight ahead.

That this guy believed LAPD had coerced a confession out of his cousin wasn't unusual. People believed what they would. It was easy to blame the police when a family member got into trouble or simply got caught. That was a big part of the trouble these days, no one wanted to take responsibility.

Lisa thought of her brother. He was an honor student and had never gotten into trouble. Bad timing had gotten him killed. Bad timing and people like the ones chauffeuring her and Johnson back to the Box. Her lips compressed together to hold back the anger she felt every time she thought of that tragedy. She'd told herself for more than a decade that she'd gotten past that painful event in her life. Her chosen career field allowed her to try to stop these kinds of lowlifes. Whatever had gone down with Johnson last year was somehow all tangled up in this world of communities within communities, each with its own laws of survival. She was now convinced more than ever that Johnson was innocent.

The question was, to what degree? He hadn't killed those three men, she was certain. But did he know who had? Was he involved on some level she hadn't considered before? Any man whose presence prompted a visit with Buster Houston represented a value of some sort on the street. Respect came at a high price in this seedy world.

What exactly had Sam Johnson purchased with his silence? A man like him, with no record and a stellar career within the law enforcement realm, didn't turn without motivation. Was protecting his family the reason for his continued silence? That would be the simplest deduction. But Lisa had a feeling that this strange alliance was anything but simple.

BY THE TIME they reached downtown L.A., Sam had mentally prepared for Smith's interrogation. She would have plenty of questions. More than he could answer, he felt certain. Considering what he'd just learned, maintaining her cooperation was essential. As soon as they were back at the hotel, he would touch base with Anders. Checking in with Battles and Call wouldn't be necessary for a few more hours. Both knew to call if anything came up.

When the driver pulled to the curb more than a dozen blocks from the hotel, Sam dragged his attention back to the here and now.

"It's almost 3:00 a.m.," Sam said to him, "I have no desire to take a multiblock stroll."

The driver swiveled his head, his hands still fastened on the steering wheel. "You're lucky to be walking at all. Now, get out."

Sam held out his hand. "Our weapons."

The driver met the gaze of one of his accomplices in the rearview mirror, then turned back to Sam, "Get out."

Sam got out of the car. When the two men in the backseat emerged, Smith scooted out right behind the guy on the passenger side. The trunk was opened, and their weapons and cell phones were returned.

"I think your boss intended for you to drop us at the hotel," Smith snapped at the taller of the two who'd kept her company in the backseat. "I'm sure he won't be happy to hear that you failed to follow his orders."

"He said to leave you the *way* we found you. He didn't say nothing about *where*." He opened the car door and got in.

The car spun away from the curb. Sam assessed the block in both directions. Empty. Dark. But that didn't mean squat in this district. The first sniff of motivation would bring trouble streaming out of the woodwork.

He shoved the weapon into his waistband at the small of his back. Smith did the same with hers. Money, weapons, two major motivating assets.

The good news was that this sidewalk was a straight shot to the hotel. The bad, that it was twelve blocks with hardly any working streetlights and the usual tents and cardboard condos. Somewhere in the distance, sirens wailed. Sweat seeped from

Sam's pores as he considered the numerous hiding places for those who liked to lie in wait for just the right moment to ambush open targets. Tourists and the lost, without gang-member status to protect them in this so-called safe zone, were no better than sitting ducks in a shooting gallery.

Sam grabbed Smith's hand. She didn't resist and started forward. Eyes straight ahead, senses on red alert, he moved quickly and deliberately toward their destination. He avoided trouble for six of those twelve blocks. But his luck failed to hold out beyond that.

"I got whatcha need, *man,*" the scraggly looking hoodlum who scooted from a stoop into their path said in what was likely a fake Jamaican accent. "Rock, weed, powder…whatever makes your fantasies come true." His clothes were ragged. His mop of hair was pulled back in a haphazard braid.

"Not interested," Sam said as he pushed past him.

But the dealer wasn't going to let it go so easily. He grabbed Sam's arm. "Just trying to do business, *man.* Ain't we all?"

When Sam would have gone for his weapon, Smith pushed between them and got in the guy's face. "That's right, man," she mocked, "we all gotta make a living. Now get out of our way."

The standoff lasted another thirty seconds before the dealer sidled back onto his stoop that fronted a dry-cleaning shop.

Smith took the lead this time, grabbed Sam's hand and pulled him along as she strode quickly toward the hotel. He glanced over his shoulder several times to make sure the guy hadn't decided to follow. For the next few minutes he allowed his thoughts to wander to the feel of her smaller hand clutching his. She was strong but soft. A nice combination. Her long, blond hair bounced with each determined stride she took. Nice hair, too.

He couldn't remember the last time he'd really paid attention to the way a woman looked. A year... longer? Now definitely wasn't the time.

In the hotel lobby, they walked straight to the bank of elevators. As soon as the doors slid closed and the car started its upward glide, she launched the interrogation he'd been anticipating since leaving the headquarters of Buster Houston.

"What did Houston say to you?" She cut him a look. "I want the truth, Sam. No more games. We could have been killed tonight. I don't know what you've got on those guys, but for some reason we got a firsthand tour of a Nation hideout and we're still breathing. I'm through waiting for you to do whatever it is you've got planned. I want the whole story *now.*"

"That's going to take some time," he offered, knowing damned well she wouldn't go for it, "and we both need some sleep right now."

"Not going to happen."

The car stopped and the doors slid open. She stormed to the room and waited for him to fish the keycard from his back pocket.

"We won't be sleeping until I know what the hell is going on."

Sam pushed the door open and waited for her to enter first. "Then it's going to be a long night."

He locked the door, slid the chain into place and went into the bathroom before she could say anything else.

After splashing some water on his face, he stared at his reflection. There was absolutely no way out of this that didn't include getting dead.

It wasn't that he couldn't bear the idea of dying. Truth was that for a long while after Anna's death he'd wished for the same. He'd gone out of his way to put himself in the line of fire, driving through neighborhoods with the highest rate of fatalities from drive-by shootings. He'd hung out in the clubs that catered to criminals. He'd practically worn a big sign that said, "Shoot me!"

But it hadn't worked. Then he'd realized how unfair that thinking was to his family. Before he'd made his decision to try living again, the three men who'd raped and murdered the woman he'd loved had gotten what they deserved.

Everything had changed then. There seemed no

escape. The cops were crawling all over him. His family was worried sick. But worst of all, L.A.'s gang world was suddenly focused on him. Talk about a hairy situation. Some had respected him for taking vengeance into his own hands. Others had despised him for daring to act like one of them.

Mainly he'd been scared to death that the wrong people would learn the truth and more people he cared about would be hurt.

He hadn't been able to concentrate on his work. He'd pretty much stopped caring about his future when Anna died.

Time was supposed to heal all wounds. But time couldn't fix this.

The only way to make this right was for someone to die.

Chapter Nine

8:20 a.m.

A sound penetrated the layer of sleep holding Lisa captive. She knew she needed to wake up, but she was so tired. So comfortable. She snuggled closer to the warmth in her bed. Her next breath brought with it the earthy scent of warm male flesh. A smile tugged at the corners of her mouth.

Sam...

A jarring vibration shattered the sweet, dreamy state where she lingered on the edge of sleep.

Her phone.

Trembling on the bedside table.

Her eyes opened.

A slice of brilliant light cut through the darkness of the room. She blinked to focus her vision. The sunlight peeked in through the parting in the drapes.

Hotel.

The Box.

She tried to sit up, couldn't, then fumbled for her phone.

A groan rumbled against her ear. She turned her head to the left and came face-to-face with Sam Johnson. His arm across her chest had her trapped against the bed. The front of his muscular body was pressed along her side, every hard, lean contour registering instantly in her brain along with the heavy male thigh draped across hers.

She licked her lips and forced her attention back to the phone, which had started to vibrate in her hand.

"Sm—" she cleared her throat "—Smith."

"Smith, are you hung over?"

Chuck Sanford. Her partner.

The man wrapped around her roused, grunted as his hand closed around her breast. Lisa's breath caught.

"Oh, hell." Chuck laughed. "Did I catch you at a bad time? I figured you'd be up by now. I'll call you later."

"No." Lisa scrambled away from Johnson, who suddenly sat bolt upright. "It's okay." She stumbled into the bathroom and closed the door. "I'm up. What's going on?" Lisa looked in the mirror, grimaced. She looked like hell. Johnson had given her just a taste of that truth she'd demanded and then he'd insisted she get some sleep. He had promised to tell her the rest this morning. The last time she roused and looked at the clock it had been around five. Evidently, he'd opted to get some shut-eye sometime after that. She shivered at the memory of his body against hers, his hand on her—

"We had a major battle over on the corner of South Western and Vernon around four this morning. We don't know all the details yet but it was bloody. The one witness who would talk says a half-dozen perps wearing red bandannas mowed down these four junkies and their dealer. The dead are all Crew."

Lisa absently rubbed at her forehead in hopes of warding off the beginnings of a headache. It was a miracle there was a witness at all. People didn't usually want to risk becoming a fatality themselves by speaking up in situations like this. Too often the gang members were people they knew, people who knew them…who knew where they lived.

"Happens all the time, Chuck," she returned, shifting her attention back to the conversation. Time to make this real. "You felt the need to call me on my vacation to tell me about this?" The suspicion in her voice made her want to bite her tongue. That guy last night—this morning actually—had her second-guessing what she knew. Her partner was a good guy. One of the best.

"You're right," he said with a heavy exhale, "I

shouldn't have bothered you on your vacation." Pause. "It's just that…"

Trepidation trickled through her. "What? Come on, Chuck, you got me up. Spill it." This indecisiveness wasn't like her partner at all.

"Their faces were marked with an X drawn in their own blood just like the three vics Johnson swore killed his fiancée."

Lisa sagged against the sink. "Gunshot victims?" He'd said they were mowed down. That generally meant gunfire. She held her breath, praying that this might be a break that pointed away from Johnson in the year old case.

"Yeah. AK-47. Not a pretty sight."

"I, ah, appreciate you letting me know. So, you think this might have a tie in to that old case?" There had to be more to this call than that.

"Maybe. Maybe not. With Watts clamoring for Johnson's head, it's hard to say what's going on. Johnson hired some fancy P.I. agency out of Chicago to serve as security for his family. The firm where he works says he's on a job in New York. I thought you'd like to know, since that case still bothers you." Another of those overdone sighs. "I guess what I'm saying is, you could be right. There could be something to the idea that Johnson didn't kill those guys."

She restrained the urge to shout *yes*. For months

she'd been telling him that there was something wrong about the case. He'd played her off every single time. That it took four more dead gangbangers to sway him wasn't good, but at least he was looking at the situation a little differently now.

The part about Johnson's current whereabouts abruptly filtered past all the rest. Chuck had been looking into where Johnson was. If word got out that he'd met with Buster Houston—with her in tow—her partner would hit the roof. She'd be suspended, and Sam Johnson would be under investigation…again.

"I won't say I told you so," she tossed back since that was what he would expect.

"Yeah, yeah, I know. Anyway, I'll let you get back to your *vacation*. I just thought you'd want to know."

"Thanks, Chuck. I appreciate it."

Lisa severed the connection and stared at her phone for a long minute. She considered the calls her partner had made to the landline at her house and his surveillance of her calls. Something was going on. Something more than he was telling her.

When she'd freshened up, she exited the bathroom to find Sam Johnson hovering outside the door. She started to rail at him for eavesdropping, but he brushed past her and closed himself up in the bathroom so fast she didn't get the chance. So maybe eavesdropping hadn't been his motive for loitering outside the bathroom door.

The need to find a deli or coffee shop gnawed at her stomach, but she ignored it. She went to the window and drew back the drape just far enough to survey the street below. The Box looked totally different by day. Gone were the tents and cardboard condos and the street people who utilized them. The cars of businessmen and women, along with delivery trucks, lined the curbs. There wasn't a single dealer slinging dope or prostitute showing off her wares. The scaffolding and Dumpsters provided a ray of hope for the future by the light of day. Long-neglected buildings were being reclaimed and rejuvenated as high-end housing.

Nothing was what it seemed. Two different worlds.

Her gaze drifted to the closed bathroom door; just as Sam Johnson was two different men. There was the focused man of science who'd once used his skills to help catch criminals, and then there was the man she'd met twenty-four hours ago…the wary, determined guy with no care for his own safety.

AK-47. Her partner had said that the victims in this morning's predawn gun battle were killed by AK47s. One of the men who'd escorted them on their midnight journey had been carrying an AK-47. Not that he would be the only thug carrying that kind of weapon on the streets of L.A. on any given night, but the fact did seem a little coincidental. Especially considering the way the victims had been marked after death.

Johnson emerged from the bathroom and she decided that now was as good a time as any for him to make good on that promise he'd made a few hours ago. She'd wanted the lowdown on his conversation with Houston at three-thirty this morning, but he'd put her off, insisting they needed to get some sleep. He'd claimed he needed to consider what he'd learned before discussing it.

He'd had four hours to consider, it was time for him to give it to her straight.

As if he'd read her mind, those gray eyes zoomed in on hers. "Let's get some coffee and talk."

It was about time.

THERE WERE PLACES in downtown L.A. that Lisa couldn't afford to be seen during daylight hours, but Coffee Joe's was not one of them. Though some areas of the Box were only a short walk from City Hall, this corner was several blocks clear of that cop sector.

With a decent breakfast behind them and a third cup of coffee steaming from their cups, Lisa had waited long enough. She'd already filled him in on the call from her partner.

"Okay, let's have it."

"Fifteen months ago I found the one spec of DNA amid a multitude of evidentiary items that placed Kenan Watts at the scene of a multiple homicide."

She knew that part. Two Los Angeles police officers had been the victims. "He got life, since we couldn't prove he was the shooter, just that he was there." The D.A. had even offered him a deal. All Watts had to do was finger the shooter and he'd get probation—as long as he had nothing to do with the shootings. He refused, which meant unless he was the shooter, one or more cop killers had gotten away scot-free.

"Two months after his indictment, Anna was murdered."

She and Chuck had gotten the case. Johnson ID'd all three perps from photographs in one of Homicide's many suspect books, and the perps were hauled in for questioning. When it came time for him to make the final identification, he insisted he couldn't be sure. Any physical evidence had been destroyed when her body was partially burned. Johnson's testimony was all they'd had. Without it they had no choice but to release the three perps.

Days later they were all three dead and marked with an X. Chuck insisted Johnson had backed out on IDing the guys so he could have his vengeance. Lisa hadn't been able to believe that...but she'd doubted herself from time to time. Like last night when he'd managed to be hosted by the leader of the Nation and walk away without so much as a wrinkle in his shirt to show for it.

"The Man paid me a visit."

The late James Watts, Kenan and Lil's uncle and only blood relative. She'd known it, damn it. Deep in her gut, she'd suspected this was the case. Lisa instinctively leaned forward. She'd waited for this for more than a year.

"He apologized for his nephew's mistake and assured me that if I kept my mouth shut that he would see that those three were properly punished." Johnson searched her eyes, his hesitation palpable. "So I did. It was the least I could do for Anna."

The woman in her wanted to cheer his decision, but the cop in her understood the ramifications of that judgment. He'd interfered with an official investigation and he'd had advance knowledge of the impending murder of three men, deserving or not. But she didn't say a word for fear he would refuse to tell her the rest.

"As promised, Watts delivered."

"And you let us bang our heads against the wall," she interjected, unable to keep the edge of bitterness out of her voice. As deeply as she understood the pain he'd been through and the probability that his decisions at the time were likely not made with a stable mental outlook, still he'd been wrong. He'd committed a crime.

"Lil Watts was furious. He was the one to order the hit on Anna, but James refused to execute his own nephew. He argued that I was responsible for Lil's brother going to prison, in a matter of speaking, and so we'd call that part even. I wasn't satisfied. I wanted Lil Watts to pay the price, as well. I couldn't think of anything else."

She recalled those days with far too much clarity. He'd worked night and day, walked around like a ghost of the man he'd once been. She'd worried that he would end up committing suicide.

"Finally James settled the issue for me. I could either leave town and stop looking for ways to get Lil, or my family would be executed. He'd given me every opportunity to put the past behind me and I refused. I wanted Lil to pay and he knew I would keep on until I nailed him for something even if I couldn't bring myself to kill him."

The revelation brought everything into perspective. "So you left L.A. to protect your family?"

He nodded, sipped his coffee. "That was our deal. I stayed clear of Lil Watts and my family would be protected."

"But the man who made that deal with you is dead now." The big picture came into vivid focus.

Johnson nodded.

That left him in a hell of a position. Without James Watts to run interference, Lil could force Johnson's hand. Could push the issue until Johnson had no choice but to surrender to him.

Or go to the police and risk being charged as an accomplice to multiple counts of homicide.

Wait.

"What about Buster Houston. Why did he get involved?" Houston surely wouldn't give one damn what happened to Lil Watts or to Sam Johnson. Houston was Watts's sworn enemy. Had he offered his protection to Johnson just to be pitted against Watts? That didn't make sense. Particularly not from a man who spouted peace and tolerance the way Houston did.

Johnson's guard went up then, setting her on edge. What the hell else could he possibly have to hide?

"Houston is prepared to help me deal with the situation on one condition."

"'Deal with the situation'?" she echoed. She didn't need a psychic connection to understand what that meant. "What's the condition?" Not that she was condoning his actions with anything Buster Houston suggested, but she needed to know what the man wanted. It seemed strange that a man that powerful in the gang world would need anything from Sam Johnson.

"He wants me to help him lure the person he believes is responsible for James Watts's death into a trap."

"Why would he do that?" Houston and Watts were enemies. Why would Houston care who killed

Watts? LAPD had assumed Watts's murder was gang related, there hadn't been any evidence to indicate otherwise.

Johnson studied his cup for a bit as if trying to decide whether he dared drink the rest.

Finally he said, "Apparently the two men had become friends in recent years. Secretly, of course."

She pushed her cup aside, done. "Why doesn't he just carry out his vengeance? If he knows the perpetrator, why does he need you? This doesn't add up, Johnson. You surely see that."

He looked directly into her eyes. "It adds up, Smith. Houston insists that the man responsible for Watts's death is a cop. This cop is part of a band of dirty cops. The two cops Kenan Watts murdered were about to ID these guys. Kenan was ordered to execute them. The only glitch was my interference, which caused Kenan to go to prison when he would have otherwise gotten off scot-free. James Watts's subsequent pronouncement that there would be no retaliation for the part I played evidently didn't go over so well, either, since someone decided to get him out of the way. This ultimately worked for all involved. Gave Lil a clear path to get at me and Lil would definitely be a lot easier to manipulate."

Stunned, Lisa couldn't speak for nearly a minute. Johnson couldn't be serious. James Watts had been an old man, one who promoted peace. To have killed him would have béen a cold-blooded act of premeditation. Something she might expect from an angry rival gang member, but she damned sure wasn't ready to blame that on one of her colleagues. Nor was she about to take some gang lord's word about a group of dirty cops.

"Are you sure he isn't setting you up, Johnson?" she argued. That was the most probable explanation. Houston had an agenda and he was playing Sam Johnson. No doubt about it.

"I'm positive. The cop he wants to bring down is not only dirty, but the ringleader of a group of several others. He's playing God and on the take big-time. Houston says he can prove it."

"Well, then," she said, fury building in her belly, "he should prove it and let the authorities deal with it." She'd heard enough of this foolishness.

Johnson's gaze never deviated from hers. "You know that's a hell of a lot easier said than done," he countered. "And this cop is no rookie. He's a seasoned veteran with serious clout."

His last statement made her nervous. "What does this have to do with you or Anna?"

"This cop is the one who set the revenge against me in motion. Kenan Watts wasn't supposed to have gone to prison. He wasn't supposed to have been nailed period. But I wouldn't stop sifting through the evidence until I found something to use against him."

She held up her hands stop-sign fashion. "All right, so there's a dirty cop. I might go along with that, but a whole band of them? That's just more than I can swallow. So who is this supposed ringleader? Houston must have told you who he suspected."

"Yeah, he told me."

Lisa waited, none too patiently. This was a new twist in the whole mess, and she wasn't sure she wanted to waste her time listening. But if *he* was listening, she had no choice.

"Sanford, your partner."

Sam had put off telling her for several hours. Ultimately he'd had no choice but to hit her with this. The look of disbelief and astonishment on her face warned that the shock was fading and the reality would set in any second.

"There is no way my partner is dirty," she charged, her lips quivering with anger, her pupils flaring with the same, "much less leading a group of other renegade cops."

"If he's not, then he has nothing to worry about."

She shook her head. "Let's just pretend for a moment that he is responsible for what happened. How do you plan to prove it, and then what do you anticipate doing about it if and when you do?"

"I just want him to admit what he's done, provide

the names of the others involved, and then you can arrest the whole lot."

She wasn't listening to any more of this. "You've lost it, Sam. That's all there is to it. I won't be a party to this insanity." She owed her partner her trust. He'd saved her life more than once.

"What about the messages he keeps leaving on your machine? Anders said he left another one this morning before he called you on your cell phone."

"That makes him a cop with good instincts, not a dirty one. I'm the one acting outside the law."

He didn't want her down on herself. "If your partner has nothing to hide, then he can stand up to a little scrutiny. And don't forget that he stationed another detective to monitor your house. Why doesn't he trust you, Smith? Is he afraid you'll talk to me and figure out the truth?"

"He's protecting me," she said quickly. "He knows I'm hung up on this case, and he wants to see that I'm okay."

"You keep telling yourself that. But I have to be realistic. My family's lives are at stake here. Sanford is up to no good, and I'm going to prove it."

"So Houston can have him killed?" Those lush lips were set in a stern line.

Sam shook his head. "So Sanford can go to prison and get what's coming to him from some of those scumbags he sent there."

Smith scooted across the seat and stood. "I have to think about this. I can't make a decision like this on the spur of the moment. I need time."

He pushed out of his seat. "Don't take too long," he suggested. "My family has been hurt enough. I don't want them to suffer anymore."

"And what about you?" she returned crisply. "Do you care what happens to you in this equation?"

"I have to check in with Anders."

He couldn't answer her question. At one time he'd thought he no longer cared, but he didn't know anymore. No matter, that was as good a place as any to end the discussion.

He knew what he had to do.

All she needed to do was see that Sanford got what was coming to him when the dust settled.

The explosion of gunshots rent the air a split second before the plate-glass window shattered. Sam took Smith to the floor with him, using his body to shield hers. Glass fragments sprayed like hail from a sudden summer storm across the floor.

Then came the eerie silence.

Chapter Ten

Screams and cries reverberated in the coffee shop as if everyone present had erupted from their paralyzing fear at the same instant. Sam came up on all fours first to assess the situation. Whoever had done the shooting was long gone. The pedestrians on the sidewalk had started to move to the window to look inside the coffee shop, hoping to get a look at the carnage.

Sirens wailed in the distance.

They couldn't be caught in here. Word would go straight to Sanford that his partner had been dining with Sam Johnson.

Sam jumped to his feet, pulling Smith up with him. "We have to get out of here."

She'd drawn her weapon and was surveying the damage. "Was anyone hurt?" she demanded as she moved away from him.

Damn it. Didn't she get it? They had to disappear before the first officers were on the scene.

Smith walked the length of the shop, checking on those just finding the nerve to crawl from under tables and from behind the counter.

The man he used to be would have done that same thing…first. When had that changed? Had the events of the last year hardened him to the point that he would walk away before checking on the innocent bystanders?

Smith shoved her weapon back into her waistband and strode quickly back to where he still stood. "No injuries." She looked around. "There has to be a back door out of here."

He nodded, then followed as she hurried around the counter and into the kitchen. The hired help had either moved to the front of the shop or were still hidden, since the kitchen was deserted. The smell of burnt muffins filled the air.

Smith eased the back door open and ensured no cops had shown up in the alley just yet.

"Clear," she muttered.

He followed her out the door, rushed along the alley until they reached the far end of the block. They dropped into a more relaxed stride as they fell into step with the pedestrians on the sidewalk running parallel to the cross street.

Sam surveyed the street and the shop fronts on either side of the road, watching for anything out of sync…any sudden moves out of other pedestrians.

A dozen cruisers had closed in on the coffee shop. Smith took a left before reaching the hotel that stood between them and the coffee shop. She weaved between three other buildings until she reached the parking lot where they'd last left the rental car.

"Do you have a destination in mind?" he asked as he unlocked the vehicle. Apparently, she'd decided to give him tit for tat. He took one last long look around to ensure they hadn't been followed.

"My place."

He hesitated but decided it was better to get into the car before pursuing any debate. "Why your place?" He started the engine and backed out of the slot as she snapped her safety belt across her lap.

She turned those brown eyes to him. "I need my computer."

"If there's still surveillance on your place, going there might not be a good idea." He paid the parking fee and pulled out onto the street.

"We'll just have to work around that obstacle. I need to access my computer."

He didn't ask why. He knew. She wanted to do some research on his accusations. Wouldn't do her any good. Sanford and his cronies were too smart to leave tracks that easy to follow. But he would indulge her for the moment.

For now, getting and staying out of sight was an excellent idea.

JOHNSON PARKED THE CAR on the street adjacent to Lisa's own. She'd lived in this neighborhood for four years. She knew the residents who worked and those who were retired. Taking care to stay close to the hedge line she moved along the driveways and back-yards belonging to those already gone for the day.

Johnson had put a call in to Anders to let him know they were approaching from the rear. Anders would keep an eye on whoever had stakeout duty today just to make sure he stayed put.

"Your partner called again," Anders said as soon as she'd cleared the back door.

"This time," he went on as she went straight to the refrigerator for a cold drink, "he remotely erased all the previous messages."

Lisa refused to allow that bit of news to influence her at the moment. There could be a plausible explanation for Chuck's behavior. If she had to guess, she'd say he was suspicious about what she was up to, and she couldn't blame him for that.

"Colby wants a conference call," Anders said to Johnson. "He wants an update on where we are."

Johnson glanced at her, then said to Anders, "We don't know where we are yet."

Lisa ignored his pointed remark. At least he hadn't shared his groundless theories about her colleagues yet. She headed for the second bed-room she'd turned into an office, not bothering to respond. Her living-room sofa was a hideaway bed, providing space for overnight guests. Not that she ever had any. She was too busy with work. But it was always better to be prepared. In all honesty, she didn't really have time for much of a social life. This was the first time off she'd taken in years.

Lately, the loneliness had gotten to her a little more than usual. But like everything else that wasn't stamped priority, she didn't have time for that right now.

She sat down at her computer and scrolled through her files until she found the one she needed. Two murdered cops. As hard as she and Chuck had worked, they'd come up with insufficient evidence to nail the perp they'd caught near the scene until Sam Johnson had found that DNA. The idiot perp had spit in the faces of his victims. But then he'd realized that might be a mistake and he'd attempted to wash their faces clean of any saliva. He'd missed a spot.

Sam's stellar forensics work had nailed a major player in the gang world. The nephew of The Man: Kenan Watts.

She studied the reports she'd prepared. All seemed in order. Then she searched her files for the next cop-killer case. Three years ago. A rookie who'd been partnered up with a veteran. He'd been off-duty. Had gone to return a couple of DVDs and gotten gunned down in the video-store parking lot. Months after the shooting, his wife had come forward and insisted that her husband had suspected some kind of trouble in his division. Priority Homicide. He'd decided to go to Internal Affairs with his suspicions, but that never happened. When asked why she'd waited so long to bring this up, she'd insisted that grief had prevented her from delving into the matter at first.

That was another case Lisa and Chuck had gotten. The perp was never found. There hadn't been a single trace of evidence. Just another unsolved homicide in the City of Angels.

The fact was, none of this meant anything. There were hundreds of murders in the L.A. area every year. Sometimes, unfortunately, the victims were cops. But that didn't mean there was a conspiracy of bad cops against good cops.

If her partner was into something like that, she would know. She wasn't that naive or that blind. The detective sitting outside her house and the constant calls to check her answering machine were only because Chuck worried about her. Charles Sanford was her mentor. Her friend.

Next she read through the news articles that had been published on the murders. The investigation had been by the book, from beginning to end. What Buster Houston was suggesting was incomprehensible.

But the detective in her wouldn't let her blindly

insist that there was no thread of believability in his accusations. The best way to disprove a lie was to find the truth.

Easy enough. Jason Rivera, the cop who'd been murdered three years ago and whose wife had insisted he had been suspicious of some of his fellow officers, was the place to start. His partner was retired now, but he was still alive. And so was Jason's widow.

Asking all the same old questions might be a waste of time, but she intended to do this right. It was too important to do otherwise. If Buster Houston intended to use her partner for some agenda, only he knew about it. She had to disprove his accusations and put a stop to his plan. The shortest route to accomplishing that was to convince Johnson that Houston was wrong…was using him.

Sam briefed Spencer Anders and Jim Colby on the events of the past fourteen hours, including the drive-by shooting which had already been reported on every single local news channel. If the police had his and Smith's descriptions, the information hadn't been released to the media.

"Just one more thing," Colby said via the speaker phone on Smith's answering machine.

Sam and Anders shared a look. Sam doubted that

Colby had learned anything he didn't already know, but his tone was grim.

"If either of you receive any orders or instructions via Battles, Call or Victoria, I want you to confirm those directly with me."

Another look passed between Sam and Anders. "Is there a problem?" Anders asked, when Sam chose not to.

Sam understood exactly what was going on here. He'd spent a lot of years reading people, mostly dead ones, but a lot of the principles were the same. Victoria Colby-Camp didn't want her son delving into hardcore cases. Sam had watched her interference increase over the past few months. Jim Colby had reached his limit on patience. Sam hated to watch this wall go up between mother and son, but one of them had to be prepared to compromise and so far he'd seen no indication of either one leaning in that direction.

"No problem," Sam assured Colby. He didn't expect to be on the receiving end of many directives. Most of his decisions were real-time in the field. There was no opportunity to run his thoughts by anyone else. Like when they'd escaped that shoot-out this morning. He'd done what he had to do.

Smith entered the room. She'd showered and changed. Her long blond hair was still damp. As he watched, she twisted it around into a bun then clamped it with a clip to hold it into place.

"I have to follow up on a couple of loose ends." She reached for her handbag and her weapon.

Sam pushed out of his chair. "I'm ready."

Her gaze connected with his. "I need to do this alone."

"Not going to happen." He tucked his own weapon into his waistband. "You didn't let me take a single step without you right on my heels. I'm claiming the same right."

"Give me an update in three to four hours," Anders reminded as they headed for the back door.

They took the same route as before from her house to the car. This time she drove. Sam waited until they'd put a few blocks between them and her house before he questioned her plan.

"Where are we headed?"

"To see Jason Rivera's partner."

So she wasn't so sure about Sanford.

"Before you form any conclusions," she said testily, "this is for you, not me. I know Charles Sanford. I'm not worried. But I need you to see that I'm right before this goes any further. And while we're both still alive."

Sounded like a waste of time to him, but he would keep an open mind. If she could make a valid case, he would weigh it against the proof Houston had. First he'd have to get the man to show it to him.

FORTY-FIVE MINUTES LATER they arrived at the Glendale residence of one Detective Roger Cornelius, retired. The man lived alone since his wife had died the year before. He was confined to a wheelchair, but looked fit for a fellow without the use of his legs.

"You're sure I can't get you two some coffee?" he asked for the third time since their arrival.

"No, thanks," Smith assured him. "We don't want to put you to any trouble."

Sam didn't remember this particular detective. He knew most in Priority Homicide, but this wasn't one he'd ever worked with on a case.

"You said you needed my help on an old case," he said to Smith, his expression bright. Every cop, no matter how old or how ill, missed the investigative work.

Smith looked completely relaxed, but Sam knew that wasn't the case. She didn't want to do this, even though she hadn't said as much. Doubting her colleagues was not something she enjoyed. The woman had a great deal of pride in her badge and all it stood for. Sam admired that about her. The years on the job hadn't jaded her, and in this city that was a hell of an accomplishment.

"Your partner Jason Rivera's murder. How did you feel about his wife's assertions that he'd been on to some illegal activities within the division?

Didn't she even insist that his suspicions were the reason he was murdered?"

Cornelius's expression fell instantly. "Why would you bring up that nonsense?"

She held out her hands as if she didn't understand it, either. "Some perp brought it up during an interview. He claims he has proof that Rivera was on to something."

Sam tensed. She was pushing it a little too close for his comfort. He hadn't given her carte blanche to come in here and give away what they knew or their source.

"Hell, Lisa, you know that's crazy." Cornelius's agitation escalated. "That woman went off the deep end when her husband was murdered. She had to blame someone and it just happened to be us. If there'd been any truth to her allegations, why didn't she bring up that crap right after he was murdered? Besides," he went on, "you know every detective in Priority Homicide. There shouldn't be any question."

"There isn't," Smith assured him, her face packed with sincerity. "But I have to follow through on something like this so it doesn't come back to haunt us. The last thing we want is some jerk mouthing off to the press and word getting around that we refused to investigate the allegations."

Cornelius considered that for a moment. "I guess

you're right. The damn media exploits everything these days. What's Sanford saying about this?"

The slightest hesitation almost gave her away, but she recovered quickly. "Do you even have to ask?"

Cornelius snorted. "Hell, no. He's probably as ticked off as I am."

Sam watched as Smith led him right to where she wanted him from there. She was a damned good interrogator.

"Rivera was your partner," she said. "You didn't get any sense that he felt there was illegal activity going on in the division?"

The retired detective shook his head adamantly. "Not a clue. If he'd ever said anything like that, I would have set him straight. I don't know what he was thinking or if he was even thinking it. You know, maybe his wife made it up. She was wrecked about his death. They had two little kids, and I think maybe she just had a nervous breakdown or something."

"Did she seek counseling? I don't recall that she pursued her allegations."

"Nope. She let it go." He shrugged. "Who knows why? Probably because it was a fabrication. But she didn't pursue it, and that was the best for everyone. There was no need to tarnish her husband's reputation or the division's."

"You spent twenty years in Homicide, Roger,"

Smith noted. "I don't think we've ever had a dirty cop. We're the cleanest division in the department and it's because of good cops like you."

"Damn straight. We keep our noses clean and do our job. End of story. Anybody who says different is a liar, plain and simple."

"Did Rivera have financial problems?"

She slid that one in while the man wasn't looking. Again Sam was impressed.

"You know…" He squinted in concentration. "Now that you bring that up, there was talk after his death that he'd gotten into a bit of a bind. But I still don't believe he was going after the division for personal gain." He waved off the whole idea. "He was my partner. I think I would've known if he was up to something like that."

"I think you're right. Thanks, Roger." Smith stood and shook his hand. "I'll make sure this rumor gets crushed. Don't you worry about that for a minute. Rivera was a fine detective."

Sam followed her out of the neat ranch-style home and to the car where she slid behind the wheel. He glanced back at the house and did a double take. For a second he'd thought he saw Cornelius watching them go. Only, he wasn't doing so from the level of a man seated in a wheelchair, he was standing up. The blind snapped closed so quickly Sam couldn't be sure.

"How was it Cornelius ended up in a wheel-chair?" he asked as Smith backed out onto the street.

"A shooting. He still has a little feeling in his legs, but not enough to permit standing or walking. The injury forced him into early retirement. Happened right after his partner was murdered."

Sam stared back at the house a moment as they drove away. Interesting: a detective who hadn't had a clue that his partner was investigating the goings-on in his own division; who had been disabled by a gunshot; and who, Sam was certain, had been standing at that window.

Noon had come and gone and Sam's stomach rumbled in protest of his negligence. The lack of sleep was catching up to him, as well. With that thought came the memory of waking up entangled with Detective Smith. Her soft body had been pressed intimately along his. He'd been having the best dream when he'd awakened. She'd been under him instead of next to him, and he'd been driving deep into her. His body tightened even now at the memory. Not exactly smart of him to dwell on a fantasy involving one of the detectives who would like nothing better than to prove he'd somehow been involved with no less than three murders.

That was one thing a guy could count on. When it came to sex, intelligence had nothing at all to do with it.

He took his time visually perusing her profile. Nice high cheekbones and full lips. Soft skin. He'd liked waking up to the smell of her.

Funny, he hadn't had the first zing of attraction other than these feelings for Smith since Anna was murdered. Just his luck to find himself in lust with the woman who was so obsessed with finding the truth about his past that she'd spend her vacation doing so.

He had a bad feeling that the truth she wanted so badly to find was not going to be what she expected. She couldn't see that sometimes the closest people hurt you the most. Maybe he was jumping the gun, but Buster Houston had no reason to lie about Sanford. This was much bigger than a simple lie.

This was going to rock LAPD. The repercussions would be felt all the way to the far sides of gangland.

"You have a question you want to ask, Johnson?"

He snapped out of the trance he'd drifted into. "Yeah…ah, where are we going now?"

"We're going to see if we can find Rivera's widow. If she was whacked out back then and talking nonsense, she should be able to admit that by now. Or, at the very least, explain it. I want to know why she attacked the division her husband loved." She braked for a light and let her gaze settle on his. "I want to know why she isn't dead already if she possessed that kind of information."

A valid point. "You know, Smith, Cornelius is

probably putting a call in to your partner to warn him as we speak."

"Maybe." She moved forward, maneuvering through the traffic. "I guess I'll cross that bridge when I come to it."

Sam had a feeling they were coming to that particular bridge a lot faster than she suspected.

Chapter Eleven

2:00 p.m.

Gloria Rivera lived in a quiet Sherman Oaks neighborhood that had found its place in the ongoing revitalization of once-crumbling communities. The small bungalow sat on a corner lot surrounded by a well-tended yard. In the driveway, a ten-year-old sedan looked a little the worse for wear.

Lisa didn't know Mrs. Rivera very well, but they had met several times during the investigation into her husband's murder. Not once had she mentioned her suspicions to Lisa. It wasn't until afterward, when the case had grown cold and she and Chuck had moved on to one of their numerous other cases that she'd heard Mrs. Rivera had gone to Internal Affairs with her allegations.

Chuck had met with the people from IA and handled the situation. Lisa hadn't been questioned.

Apparently, not enough grounds to pursue the investigation had been found. As far as Lisa had known, that was where it ended. A grieving widow seeking someone to blame.

But could she have been wrong about that? Could there have been more, and she just didn't know about it? That would mean her partner had left her out of the loop on some of the details.

Innocent until proven guilty. Even the most heinous criminals got that benefit of the doubt. Why wouldn't her partner, her division, be worthy of the same?

"I'll do the talking," she reminded Johnson. She didn't need him taking off on his own agenda. She was the one with the badge, even if the investigation was unofficial.

"I'll do the listening," he said, with far more humility than she knew him to possess.

The impulse to tell him what she thought of his patronizing almost got the better of her, but she managed to resist the temptation.

A jungle-gym decorated in brilliant primary colors dominated the side yard. Two kids…who'd lost their father. She swallowed back the sickening sensation that accompanied the thought.

Lisa pressed the doorbell and waited. Canned laughter and the familiar antics of a kids' program blared from a television set inside. Good sign. Somebody was most likely home.

The wood door opened and a thirtyish Hispanic woman peered through the screen door first at Sam then at Lisa. She hesitated for a moment, then said, "I remember you."

"Mrs. Rivera, I'm Detective Lisa Smith. I have a few questions for you if you don't mind."

Another of those troubled hesitations and uncertain glances, first at the man standing next to Lisa then at her. "What kind of questions? What's this about, Detective?"

Shouting from inside signaled two or more children were not happy with each other. The indignant cries for "Mom" confirmed the theory.

"Excuse me," Mrs. Rivera said before rushing off to calm the storm.

A few moments later she returned to the door. "What do you want?" The surprise was gone, only annoyance and maybe some amount of suspicion remained.

"Mrs. Rivera, there are a couple of things unclear about the statement you gave to Internal Affairs three years ago. I'd like to review your statement with you. See if we can't resolve the questions."

"There's nothing to resolve," she snapped, both hands settling on her hips. "My husband was murdered by one of you." Fury glittered in her eyes. "Maybe you didn't get your hands dirty by actually pulling the trigger, but one of you ordered his execution. I don't care what anyone says. That's the truth."

Lisa carefully schooled her reaction. She couldn't let the woman see the shock or the disbelief. "Ma'am, I'm sorry if you've had a difficult time with making yourself understood, but that's why I'm here now. I'd like to change that, if you have the time to discuss the matter now."

Hesitation lingered in her eyes. "All my friends say I should just let it go. But I can't. I have to live with that every day. Knowing that his own people killed him and nobody cares." She unlocked the screen door and stepped back. "Come in."

When Mrs. Rivera had settled the children for the second time, she returned to the living room where Lisa and Johnson waited. She sat down directly across from Lisa and folded her hands in her lap.

"What do you want to know?"

"Did your husband ever talk about any problems he might be having with one or more gang members?"

A frown furrowed her brow. "No. We didn't really discuss his work that often. But the last couple of months of his life he kept talking about requesting a transfer. He said we'd sell the house and move to Pasadena or some place. Anywhere away from L.A."

"Did he mention to you what was troubling him?" Funny, she didn't remember any discontent in Rivera at work. He'd done his job—quite well, at that—and he'd talked about his kids.

"He said there were things going on that he didn't approve of. He'd been approached to participate, but he refused. It was supposed to be okay except the others started acting funny toward him. Made him feel as if he didn't belong." Tears shone in her eyes as she said the last.

"But he didn't give you any specifics on what he meant by things going on?"

She shook her head. "Just that they were getting paid to look the other way. He didn't talk about it a lot, but I could tell it weighed on his mind."

"He didn't mention any names?"

"No. Sometimes he'd rattled off a few names. They might have been gang members. Nothing specific."

Pain and grief had routed out deep lines at the corners of her eyes. She looked tired, perhaps from playing both mother and father.

"If you were so certain that something was going on in our division, why didn't you push the issue? Why let it go so easily, Mrs. Rivera?" It was clear to Lisa, sitting there face-to-face with the lady, that she was a fighter. She was giving everything she had to raise her children and take care of the home. Her deceased husband's pension and life insurance had evidently allowed her to remain a stay-at-home mother. Why would a fighter give up so easily?

As if she'd suddenly remembered an appointment, Mrs. Rivera stood. "You should go. I've said too much already. What does any of it matter now? My husband is dead. Nothing I do is going to give my children their father back."

Lisa pushed to her feet. Johnson followed suit. "Mrs. Rivera, you don't need to be afraid to speak with me about anything that troubles you."

She searched Lisa's eyes, seemed to hesitate, but then changed her mind. "It took me a while to get up my nerve to go to someone about what I knew after my husband was murdered, and it was a mistake. I got the message," she said quietly. "If this is some sort of trick to see if I'll say any more than what I've just told you, it's not going to work. I won't risk my children's lives like that."

"I can assure you—"

"Go," she insisted. "I can't help you."

Sam touched Lisa's arm. "Come on, let's go."

She didn't want to. She wanted to stay until this woman told her the whole truth. She needed names, dates, incidents.

She needed more than this simmering suspicion.

"Thank you, Mrs. Rivera," she said before leaving.

The widow didn't respond. She closed and locked the door behind them without another word.

Lisa strode to the car, her anger building with each step. At the driver's door she glared at Johnson across the roof of the car. "That doesn't prove anything. It's hearsay. Irrelevant."

"You're right."

With that out of the way, he got into the car and closed the door.

He said nothing else during the trip back to the hotel. She didn't ask him if that was where he wanted to go. Their options were limited. Going back to her place more than absolutely necessary was too risky. But there was one thing that wouldn't wait any longer: it was after two and she was starving. A detour through a drive-through took care of that problem.

Disgust settled heavily in her stomach along with the chicken sandwich. She'd been back in L.A. for more than twenty-four hours and she knew nothing. She was slightly closer to that truth she sought, but not nearly as close as she would like to be. And the closer she got…the more confusing everything seemed.

That she'd been right about Johnson's innocence didn't give her much comfort right now. She needed to know who killed those men if she was going to convince her partner of Johnson's innocence.

And now all this dirty-cop business had come up.

Lisa stuffed another French fry into her mouth. She refused to lend any credence to Sam and Houston's allegations regarding her partner. She would need a lot more than some gang lord's conspiracy theories. Or the suspicions of a man who carried a serious grudge.

She parked in the usual spot, and Johnson marked the windows with his borrowed bar of soap. It seemed inconceivable that something as insignificant as soap drawings would protect their car. But so far it had worked.

The lobby was deserted. Silent as a tomb.

Sam didn't like the fact that the guy who was usually behind the counter was missing. Granted the place wasn't that busy, but to leave the desk unmanned seemed a little peculiar.

As they reached the elevator the hairs on the back of his neck stood on end.

Johnson grasped Lisa's arm, drawing her to a stop. "Something's wrong," he said as he surveyed the empty lobby once more.

"Yeah, I feel it, too. Something's off."

"You stay down here." He inclined his head toward the desk. "Maybe behind the counter. I'll go up to the room and check things out."

"Bad strategy. It's you they want. You lay low behind the desk. I'll go up."

"I'm not having you killed in my stead."

The way he looked at her when he made that statement sent a shiver through her. Her safety being important to him—really important—touched her. She stabbed the call button for the elevator.

"Don't be ridiculous. If there's an ambush waiting for us, you know they're not going to kill me until they know where you are. I'll be perfectly safe."

Sam didn't like letting her go, but she had a point and one of them had to do this. She also had a gun and knew how to use it.

"Behind the counter," she ordered as the elevator doors slid open.

"I'll keep an eye on the elevators and the main entrance," he told her before following her order. "If you're not back in five minutes, I'm coming up."

He didn't give her a chance to argue. He hustled over to the front desk and took a position out of sight.

Lisa stepped into the elevator, and the doors glided shut. Her heart rammed into triple time. She checked her weapon at the small of her back. No need to be nervous. Even if Lil Watts himself were up there, she would be safe until they learned Johnson's location.

She exited the elevator and walked to the door of her room. The keycard in hand, she'd just attempted to insert it when the door burst open.

"Detective Smith."

Three of LAPD's finest from Priority Homicide Division waited in the room.

"What's going on, Jessup?" She looked to the detective she knew best, Bruce Jessup. Not that she knew any of these three particularly well, but Jessup was one she'd worked with before.

"That's what we want to know," Scruggs said from his position behind Jessup.

"Just answer a few questions and everything will be fine, Lisa," Jessup urged.

With the door closed behind her, the taller of the two remaining detectives, Tony Hicks, began the inquisition.

"When did you return from Cozumel?"

"Yesterday," she lied.

"Why are you staying in this hotel?"

Now that she took the time to look around the room she had to wonder the same. "My lover didn't want to go anywhere he might be recognized." That at least was partially true.

"We have two witnesses," Hicks said, "who can place you with Sam Johnson just a few hours ago."

"I don't know what you're talking about," she argued, infusing surprise into her tone, as well as her expression. The idea that these guys could be the dirty detectives Rivera's wife had told her about blinked in her head like a caution light. *Impossible,* part of her argued.

A knock on the door signaled a new arrival. God, she hoped it wasn't Johnson. He'd said he would give her five minutes. Jessup opened the door.

Lisa's jaw dropped when her partner walked into

the room. Somewhere beyond the shock, she was glad it wasn't Johnson.

"What's going on here, Chuck?" Now maybe she'd get some straight answers.

Her partner jerked his head toward the door and the others exited the room. Another rush of tension sent adrenaline charging through her veins.

When the door had closed, Sanford lit into her. "What the hell are you doing, Lisa?"

"I don't know what you mean." She worked hard to keep the expression on her face neutral.

"I knew you were obsessed with this case—with Johnson. But to lie to me about going to Cozumel when you never even left the country, that's just going too far."

Guilt pinged her. She'd let her partner down. Left him in the dark.

"I just needed some time to think."

"You're making a mistake, Lisa," he said. "I wish you wouldn't do this."

For the first time since she'd met Charles Sanford, his words felt like a threat…a warning.

"If I do this, whatever you think *this* is, just what's going to happen?" She didn't back off when his glower darkened.

"Johnson is guilty, if not of murder, of something. I don't know why you're taking up with him like this, but it's a slap in the face to all of us at Homicide.

You'll regret what you're doing. Go take that vacation you lied to me about. That'll do you a hell of a lot more good than this."

He pivoted and headed for the door.

"What about Rivera? Did he regret what he'd done? Is that why he's dead?"

Sanford stopped, turned back to her, and the danger in his eyes stole her breath right out of her lungs.

"This is my final warning. Take that time off… get your head on straight."

After he'd gone, Lisa waited until the count of ten before leaving the room. Gave Sanford and his buddies time to get out of there. If she waited much longer, Johnson would come to check on her. He might run into her partner or one of the others.

She wasn't ready for that to happen yet.

Instead of taking the elevator, she took the stairs. She leaned over the railing and looked and listened. Clear. She took each flight in a near run. As she hit the second-floor landing, the door leading into the corridor burst open.

Her brain barely had time to acknowledge that it was Sam before he dragged her into the corridor.

"You were supposed to stay out of sight," she snapped.

"Yeah, well, I never was any good at following orders."

"We need to get out of here," she told him. She

had a bad feeling that their next visitors might not leave so easily and without the exchange of gunfire.

"I thought I recognized one of Priority Homicide's finest. Did your partner show up?"

The question shouldn't have annoyed her.

"Yes."

"What did he say?"

"He said I was making a mistake and that I should take the vacation I'd lied to him about." More of that infuriating frustration whipped through her. He'd basically threatened her and then he'd acted as if nothing at all untoward had happened.

Johnson hesitated halfway to the elevators on the second floor. "Ask yourself, Smith, why would he track you down like this? What's he really worried about?"

She lifted her chin in defiance of what he wanted her to say, what her mind wouldn't let her pretend away. "I don't know, but whatever it is, it has something to do with you. At this point I figure if I stay with you, the whole thing will go down eventually. Maybe then we'll have some answers."

He guided her to the door behind her, shoved a keycard into the door's lock and opened it. When had they changed rooms?

"We have a different room now?"

He shook his head. "The other room is still ours. We need to get a couple of hours' sleep before night falls and the guardians of the turf come out in full force. I have a feeling we're going to be very popular tonight."

"We're already popular," she muttered.

This room had two queen beds. How nice. He'd made sure they didn't have to sleep together again. She doubted she would sleep, anyway.

He stripped off his shirt and shoes and stretched out across one bed. She kicked off her shoes and crawled onto the other. If she could make her brain stop for just a little while she might actually get some sleep.

What the hell was going on with her partner? How could she have worked with him for five years and missed that something was not as it should be?

This was insane.

What was even crazier was the idea that, as fired up as she was about the visit from her partner tonight, she found herself studying Johnson's form. Long muscular arms. Heavy, lean legs. The remembered feel of him had her tingling in places that had nothing to do with anything but Sam Johnson.

How were they going to figure out this puzzle? They couldn't go to anyone for help. Outside their team there wasn't anyone they could trust.

It was just the two of them, with Lil Watts and his thugs coming at them from one side while law enforcement came from the other. Sanford had to be worried or he wouldn't have bothered keeping track of her whereabouts. That had to be the reason he was having her watched. The notion that he was a cold-blooded killer was ludicrous.

Her eyes started to drift shut, but she fought it. She needed to think, to sort some of this out. She doubted Lil Watts would wait beyond the coming night. He knew Johnson was back. He was likely the one behind the drive-by shooting. He would be anxious to finish this.

If they could just survive one more night, they might be able to get some more answers from Buster Houston. He had offered this deal of luring the dirty cop. But in order to go along with that, she needed more information. She needed facts. Specific data.

Until then, she wouldn't call her partner dirty. Yeah, he was overzealous about Sam Johnson's guilt, but did that make him dirty? He could merely be reacting to her actions.

But that explanation felt less and less likely.

And left her with one major sore spot.

How had she been so blind?

Her gaze settled on Johnson once more. He was the one thing in all this that she'd been right about.

A realization settled heavily onto her just then. It was her responsibility to see that he survived this. She was a cop, Homicide. She wasn't about to allow an innocent civilian to be murdered on her watch. One might say he wasn't so innocent, since he had made no move to stop James Watts from overseeing the execution of the vengeance on those three men. But that had been out of Johnson's hands to a great extent. Watts would have done it with or without Johnson's knowledge. The same way he would use him now, with or without his knowledge.

Johnson needed protecting. Just like his family.

The best way for her to accomplish that goal was to allow him to believe that he was protecting her. He'd keep her close without argument.

With that decision out of the way, she let her lids drift closed.

Tonight was going to be a long one.

Chapter Twelve

Central Los Angeles
8:45 p.m.

Crew territory. Central L.A., Forty-eight Street through Seventy-fifth, Western Avenue to Overhill Drive. Twenty-seven blocks with over 1600 active gang members. And somewhere in this maze of neighborhoods and shops was the headquarters of Lil Watts.

Sam had parked along the curb in a busier section in hopes of avoiding trouble. Smith waited quietly in the passenger seat. That she was here at all spoke volumes about just how much she had decided to trust Sam. He wasn't sure he'd ever be able to adequately repay her.

They had taken the risk and rendezvoused with Anders. Sam hadn't slept at all. Instead, he'd laid out a plan that would, if they were lucky as hell, work. Anders agreed that it was the only way, but

Smith didn't like it. Yet she'd agreed to back him up—to a point.

The only way to get Watts off Sam's back was to kill him or send him to prison, and even the latter was no guarantee he wouldn't order executions from behind bars.

What Sam really needed was a major shake-up involving LAPD and the media. Buster Houston would help keep gangland under control after the shake-up. His influence carried a lot of weight— with everyone but Lil Watts. With Watts out of the way, some sort of peaceable arrangement could be reached once more.

Sam was reasonably sure Watts's ego and confidence were overinflated by his in with the cops. Working directly with the boys in blue, he had no fears. His predecessors would never have formed an alliance with cops. Various gang leaders of the past had at times come to understandings with law enforcement but never an alliance of "you scratch my back and I'll scratch yours" like this one appeared to be. But most of that was speculation at this point. What they needed was evidence.

In reality, all Sam had to go on was the word of Buster Houston. Well, and the odd behavior of Charles Sanford.

Time was short. Sam knew he couldn't possibly expect to last much longer without disappearing completely, and then his family would pay the price. He had to act fast with a plan that, admittedly, posed some major risks to all involved.

He needed to make Lil Watts believe that his cop allies had double-crossed him. Sam also needed Buster Houston to publicly stand up against Watts and his secret alliance that benefited no one but Watts.

Smith had accessed the LAPD system to get anything she could on recent gang activities.

Now, armed with minimal knowledge and Smith's .22, Sam's 9 mm and a high-powered rifle Anders had provided, they were almost ready to put the first phase of their plan into motion. The final piece of information they needed was a location. That would be coming any minute.

Sam's cell phone vibrated. He slid it out of his pocket and checked the display. This was the call he'd been waiting for.

"Johnson."

He listened carefully as the address was rattled off. He knew it wouldn't be repeated. The connection was severed, and he turned to Smith. "Got it."

"So we're ready," she said without making eye contact.

"We're not going to do this your way, Detective," he warned. She could raise all the holy hell she wanted. But the decision had been made. Anders and Colby agreed. Sam would be the one to go in, not her.

"If you go in there," she said, finally meeting his eyes, "you're a dead man."

He shifted his attention forward. "To some, I'm already a dead man."

"Funny."

She had this theory that because she was the cop she was supposed to take the risk. Not going to happen on his watch.

"Let's just do it my way and get it over with," he said, "Debating the issue any longer is just wasted effort."

"Look," she snapped, "*if* there's any truth to these allegations about some of the cops in my division, I want to know it. I can't get that done with you dead." She huffed a breath of frustration. "I need you."

The corners of his mouth tilted before he could stop the reaction. "I'm sorry—" he rested his gaze on hers "—I don't think I heard that last part. Could you repeat that please?"

"Go to hell, Johnson."

The amusement he'd felt temporarily vanished. "I can't allow you to risk your life for me." That was the bottom line.

"Don't flatter yourself. It won't be for you. I need to do this for me. For what I believe in."

"For your brother?" he suggested, searching her face and then her eyes when she finally met his once more.

"Sure." She lifted one shoulder, let it drop. "I'm a cop because of him. But—" she pressed Sam with a look that made it clear just how serious she was "—mainly this is about me doing my job."

His gaze narrowed with the new question that bobbed to the surface of all the other troubling thoughts churning around in his head. "You knew something wasn't right when you went to the Colby Agency." The notion had been kicking around in the back of his head since he'd walked into Victoria Colby-Camp's office and found Smith there. This was the first time he'd gone so far as to say it out loud.

"Yeah. I guess I did."

"It's tough." He watched the pedestrians on the street hurrying to get home, now that darkness was almost upon them. "You want to believe in people, in the system. But sometimes one or both fail you. It's hard to know who or what to trust."

"Whether or not I can trust my partner is still up in the air. But there's one thing you can count on— *you* can trust me."

He turned to look at her, wished he hadn't. He'd been pretending for a long time that she didn't really care about him. That he was just another case. But he'd been lying to himself. He'd seen *this* in her eyes before. Had felt that spark between them.

"I think maybe I can," he admitted.

They might never be totally on the same side, but

he knew he could trust her. She'd earned that acknowledgment the hard way, by risking her life to help him survive this long.

"We should get into position."

She was right. He started the engine and pulled out onto the street. The first step was to find a house or apartment they could use close to ground zero. He couldn't risk driving down the block where Lil Watts maintained his headquarters. After surveying possibilities on all sides of the location, he found a workable location one street over. A four-story building for lease. The front of the building he'd selected faced the back of the house that sat directly across the street from the target, giving Sam a direct view of the front of Watts's headquarters. He and Smith would get into position here while Spencer Anders tailed Sanford to make sure he didn't get in the way and to keep tabs on his whereabouts until this thing went down at noon tomorrow.

After parking in the alley that ran between the building and a long line of abandoned shops, they emerged from the car, keeping a close watch in all directions. He didn't need any of Lil's scouts to spot them. Sam took the duffel with the tools he would need from the backseat. Smith grabbed the case that contained the rifle.

The alley entrance provided the best scenario for breaking and entering. Sam retrieved the necessary tools for picking the lock and had the door open in less than half a minute. Flashlights in hand, they entered the building.

An open center stairwell led upward. On the third floor they moved to the front of the building and found the window with the best view. Since the window sashes were painted shut, he used a glass cutter to remove the glass in the lower sash. Smith assembled the high-powered rifle Anders had sent along.

She handed the rifle to Sam and he checked the target through the night-vision scope. Two of Watts's men loitered on the front porch. Sam could see them as clearly as if they were standing right in front of him. Satisfied with the preparations, he leaned the weapon against the wall next to the window.

"Last chance," he said to her. "It's not too late to change your mind. I can deliver the message."

She shook her head. "We've been over this before. It's this way or no way."

"I guess this is it, then."

She nodded and shoved Sam's 9 mm into her waistband and hung the lanyard around her neck so that her badge was displayed in plain sight against her white blouse. "I'll be back in fifteen minutes max."

When she turned to go, he said, "There's just one thing."

Smith paused, looked back at him. "Yeah? What's that?"

He shouldn't have. Hell, he was a fool to do it, but he couldn't help himself. He grabbed her by the shoulders and kissed her hard on the mouth. She tasted soft and sweet, like the chocolate she'd eaten before they left her house. He hadn't kissed a woman in more than a year and he wanted to kiss her on and on, but that would have to wait until this was over. He wanted to explore this thing between them…if she was willing.

"Be careful." He released her, stepped back.

She nodded jerkily then pivoted and headed for the stairwell.

Sam watched her go until she'd disappeared into the darkness, then he took up his position at the window.

Just don't let her get killed, he prayed.

LISA SAT IN THE CAR a moment before starting the engine. Her heart wouldn't slow its frantic beating. She couldn't catch her breath.

He'd kissed her.

She didn't know whether to whoop for joy that he actually had noticed this thing between them, or to be ticked off that he obviously believed he wouldn't be seeing her again.

That was something she'd have to ask him when she got back. And she was coming back. No way was she letting one of these slimeballs take her life.

She had too much to do.

After driving down the block, she made the turn onto the street where Watts's latest headquarters was reported to be. Anders had reached out to his own private sources and gotten the address when LAPD couldn't. She cut her department some slack; their hands were tied in many ways whereas a civilian could cross lots of lines if he had the means.

This was the place. Fourth house on the right. She pulled over to the curb, took another long, deep breath and got out.

Three black SUVs and one white Caddy lined the curb in front of the ranch-style house. The two guards on the porch had already started down the steps, weapons drawn.

Stay calm. No sudden moves.

The two men started laughing as she crossed the street in their direction.

"Is this a bust, baby?" one of them asked with a snort of derision.

"I need to talk to Lil Watts." She kept her arms hanging loosely at her sides in a nonthreatening manner as she neared their position. She looked each man in the eyes, first the one who'd spoken, then the other.

"You'd have better luck talking to Santa Claus. Now get on outta here," the second man barked, "before we find a better use for you."

"This is official business, gentlemen. Tell him that Detective Charles Sanford sent me." That the last part rolled off her tongue so easily was testament to the idea that all she'd heard the past twenty-four hours had influenced her thinking far more than she'd wanted it to.

A look passed between the two men. The guy who'd made the Santa Claus remark said, "This better be legit." He held out his hand. "Gimme your piece."

"I don't think so." She held her ground, knowing this could be the last damned thing she did.

"Suit yourself. We wouldn't want a member of L.A.'s finest to be put out," he sneered. "But make a move for it and you're dead."

"Fair enough," she allowed.

Her escorts led the way onto the porch. One pounded on the door with his fist and the door opened instantly.

"What?" The man who stood on the threshold glared at the two scouts then at her. "What you want?"

"She says she's got a message from Sanford."

A chill crawled up her spine. She couldn't possibly deny that these guys knew her partner. If that meant what it appeared to, then she'd been one big, dumb fool. Frustration and anger kindled in her belly. How could she have been so damned blind?

The guy on the other side of the threshold jerked his head for her to enter. She walked into the house, and the door slammed behind her. That Sam wouldn't be able to see her any longer made her stomach clench. She was on her own now.

"Sit."

She lowered into the closest chair. Three other men lounged on the sofa, one was cleaning his weapon, the other two were playing cards.

The guy who'd allowed her entrance left the room. She watched the seconds tick by on the wall clock. Nearly a minute and about two hundred thuds of her heart later, he returned.

"This way."

She followed him down a narrow hall and into what might have at one time been a couple of bedrooms at the rear of the house. The dividing wall had been taken out, leaving one wide-open space. Lil Watts was draped on a sectional sofa, a half-naked woman on either side of him. He looked Lisa up and down, then gave the ladies a nudge, and the two left the room. Both gave her the evil eye as they passed.

"You got some nerve walking in here like this." He adjusted the shiny chains around his neck. "What is it Sanford wants now? I told him not to be jerking me around no more. I'm The Man now. I won't be taking no more monkey-do orders from him."

Another of those icy chills went through her. "In that case, I'm afraid you're not going to like this message."

Watts pulled a pearl-handled .40 caliber gun from under the loose cushion next to him. "You sure you wanna deliver it?"

"Hey," she gave him a look that said whoa. "I'm just the messenger. If you don't like the message, tell it to Sanford."

He assessed her a long moment. "Maybe I will. He didn't say nothing about recruiting you. When did that happen? I thought you was one of them goody two-shoes cops that still thinks the world is worth saving."

"I got over it."

He laughed. "Needed a raise in pay, huh? You cops don't get paid squat."

She managed a halfhearted smile. "That's for sure."

"So what the hell does Sanford want?"

"He needs you to meet him at noon tomorrow. Corner of South Western and Vernon. An abandoned place called Soupy's."

Watts sent one eyebrow high up his forehead. "That's a little public, ain't it? We usually do our business in a more private setting."

"You want to call him and verify the time and place?" she asked, her tone impatient. She could not let him see her sweat.

His eyes tapered into assessing slits as if he was weighing her suggestion then he shrugged. "Nah. If that fool wants to meet out in the open like that, then so be it. I ain't the one with nothing to worry about." He cocked his head and studied her a moment longer. "Is this about that fool Johnson? That man's dead. Sanford don't need to be worrying 'bout that. I gave the order. He'll probably be dead before the sun comes up on another day."

Lisa shook her head. "I don't think it's about him." Then she opened her mouth as if she intended to say more, but snapped it shut, blinked twice as if uncertain. "That's all." She turned to the door, but he spoke before she could take the first step.

"You have something else on your mind, *Detective?*"

She shifted back to face him, shook her head. "No."

A frown worked its way across his brow. "I think you do."

The man who'd escorted her to the room stepped closer in an act of intimidation.

"I could get in major trouble for saying anything…. It's just that I have a big problem with what he's got planned for you."

Watts rocketed to his feet, fury contorting his face. "Explain yourself fast or one of my boys'll be cleaning your brains off that wall. How's that for major trouble?"

She held up her hands for him to back off. "Sanford and his boys are finished doing business with you. He's planning a switch to Houston. There's going to be a war and you're going to lose."

Rage blazed in his eyes. "Why should I believe that crap? Sanford knows better than to pull anything like that on me. I got too much on that bastard."

"Maybe that's the problem." She backed up a step, bumped into the other guy. She wanted these two to think she was scared. Truth was, she was pretty damned terrified. "Listen, I wouldn't really care, but it was one of Houston's people that killed my brother. I don't have any desire to do business with him or his Nation."

For three beats she wasn't sure if he'd bought it. Then he said, "You tell Sanford I'll be there. Soupy's. I know the place. If what you say is going down, then maybe me and you can do business directly in the future."

She nodded, would have turned away again but he went on. "You keep this part of our talk to yourself. You take care of me, and I'll be sure you don't ever have to worry about working with Buster Houston."

This time she gave him a real smile. "Works for me."

"Why don't you tell me exactly what Sanford's planning?"

Her tension ratcheted up. She hadn't prepared for this part. She'd just have to wing it.

"Come on, come on," Sam muttered.

She should have been out of there by now.

Two minutes more and he was going over there. If it blew the plan then it would just have to blow it.

A creak behind him had him executing an about face.

"Put down the rifle."

Four men formed a line and moved closer to his position, their weapons leveled on him.

Well, so much for holding up his end of the plan. Lisa was still in there and he wasn't going to be any help at all.

"Put down the weapon!" the leader repeated.

Sam propped the rifle against the wall, considered going for the .22 on the window ledge.

"Don't move or you're dead," the one giving the orders said, settling Sam's indecision. "Get the rifle and the handgun," he said to one of his cohorts.

One of the men stepped forward and took possession of the rifle, holding it gingerly with gloved hands. Another patted Sam down and snagged the .22 on the window ledge, then stepped back into line with his pals.

"Do it," the leader ordered.

Sam braced for the impact of bullets.

But no weapons fired.

Instead, three of the lowlifes rushed him.

He dodged the first punch. Wasn't so lucky with the

second. Before he could get in a blow of his own, one of the men had manacled his arms behind his back.

The next several punches landed in his gut.

He tried his best to block the rest of the blows from registering, but his luck didn't hold out for that, either.

Chapter Thirteen

Lisa's hands were shaking when she got back into the rental car.

She'd gotten through the meeting without getting shot or otherwise damaged.

Taking a deep breath, her first since before she'd gone into that house, she started the engine and drove away. The one-block drive to reach the building where Sam waited seemed to take forever when it was in reality less than a minute.

The side-entrance door stood open, propelling her senses to a higher level of alert. She'd closed it. Had Sam decided to go after her?

Damn. That could be disastrous.

She shoved the gearshift into Park and jumped out of the car. Flashlight. She had to have a flashlight. She ran back to the car, got the flashlight then sprinted into the building.

The silence had her pulse racing. She wanted to

call out his name, but that could alert anyone who might be prowling around in here. She took the stairs quietly, but rapidly. When she hit the third-floor landing she knew there was trouble. He should have called out to her by then.

Silence.

"Sam?"

She ran the flashlight's beam over the window. No Sam. No weapons. Slowly she swung it back and forth over the floor beyond where she stood.

The light hit the soles of his sneakers first.

Fear charged through her.

"Sam!"

She was on her knees at his side before she'd realized she'd moved. He was breathing. Thank God. She ran the light over the back of his head, his torso, then his legs. No blood, no apparent injuries.

"Sam." She leaned closer to him, directed the flashlight on his face. She grimaced. His face was bloody. Eyes swollen.

A sound echoed from somewhere in the building. She drew her weapon and sent the light over the open space around her. Nothing she could see. When she was satisfied that no one was creeping about on that floor at least, she attempted to rouse him again. She had to get him out of here. Slowly he came awake. She helped him to roll over and then sit up. His lip was cut open. His nose had stopped bleeding and didn't appear to be broken.

"What happened?" she asked as she assisted him to his feet. He was unsteady even with her help. She shifted the beam of light to the area around the window once more. "Where are the weapons and the duffel?"

"The guys who beat the crap out of me took them."

In this neighborhood she wasn't surprised at that. She was, however, a little startled that he'd let someone sneak up on him like that.

They could talk about that later.

"We have to get out of here." She guided him to the stairs, checked with the flashlight to see that the coast was clear, then started downward.

He stumbled but caught himself.

"Careful." She tightened her arm around him.

She didn't relax until she had him in the passenger seat of the car. She raced around the hood and got behind the wheel. Her fingers shook as she twisted the key in the ignition. The faster they got out of here the better.

Flooring the accelerator, she barreled out of the side alley and onto the street. Thankfully there wasn't any traffic. She didn't turn on her headlights until she'd reached the main cross street.

"Do you need a doctor?"

She could only see the surface injuries, and

judging by the way he was holding his gut, there could be far worse things going on.

"No." He groaned, grabbed his ribs.

"Okay, that's it. I'm taking you to the E.R."

"I'm okay," he growled. "Just find a drugstore. I'll tell you what I need."

Her nerves were shot and she lacked the energy to argue with him so she did as he said. She'd hit the Strip before she found a drugstore that was open this late. Parking was a pain in the rear but she managed.

"What do you need?"

"Get me some kind of pain reliever, peroxide and whatever else you think we could use."

She didn't like this. At the academy she'd had basic first aid, but there could be something serious going on that wasn't visible.

"What about your abdomen and chest? You don't feel there's any internal injuries?"

He exhaled a pained breath. "No. Some bruising for sure, but I don't think it's worse than that."

She could sit here and debate with him or she could just trust his judgment. Arguing would only waste time.

"I'll be right back."

She locked the car and hurried inside.

Fighting the urge to grab a basket and run down the aisles, she walked at a leisurely pace. One by one she gathered the items she felt might be needed.

She picked up a couple of energy bars and some bottled water. After reviewing the items she'd selected, she took a moment to compose herself. She noticed the dried blood on her right hand and reminded herself to use her left, then headed for the checkout counter.

"Will that be all?" the clerk asked.

Lisa managed a tight smile. "That's it." She dug through her purse until she found her wallet while the clerk rang up the items. Her debit card in her left hand, she waited for a total.

The television mounted to the wall behind the counter snagged her attention. The sound had been muted, but she didn't need to hear the news bulletin for her brain to register the impact.

Yellow tape, pulsing blue lights, and a news man standing in the foreground while cops swarmed what looked like someone's front yard behind him. The breaking news crawler read: Three male victims pronounced dead after a shootout. An all-points bulletin has been issued for Samuel Johnson, Jr. and a female accomplice.

The concept of what she was seeing didn't fully penetrate the shock swaddling her brain until Sam's picture flashed on the screen.

"You can swipe your card now," the clerk said.

Lisa jerked her attention back to the woman. "I'm sorry." Her hand shaking again, she swiped her card, then entered her PIN number.

The clerk stuck the receipt in the bag and thrust it at her.

Lisa hurried out of the store. The overwhelming sensation of being watched washed over her, but she was certain it was her imagination. She hurried to the car and got behind the wheel. She passed the bag to Sam.

"We have to—"

"Anders just called," he interrupted. "They've issued an APB for me and my female accomplice related to some shootout over on Fiftieth."

"I know." That meant they couldn't go back to the hotel, couldn't go to her place. And definitely couldn't use her credit cards.

Her debit card.

Damn. She'd just used it in the drugstore.

She checked her side mirror then squealed away from the curb. Calm down, she ordered. The last thing she wanted to do was get pulled over for speeding or reckless driving.

"We need a place to hide," she mumbled, talking more to herself than to him. He didn't answer. Every patrol car she passed on the street had her fingers clamping more tightly around the steering wheel. This rental car wasn't in her name, but it was in the Colby Agency's name. Her partner knew a Chicago agency was here working on Sam's case.

Not good. Not good at all.

Her parents were out of town on vacation. Going there would be too risky. But that wouldn't be a problem with the Miller house. The Millers were her parents' best friends. They vacationed together every year. That could work.

"I have an idea."

Sam was too busy trying to open the childproof cap on the pain relievers to question what she'd decided. She took the scenic route through the Hollywood Hills. The Millers had a home overlooking the city; a gorgeous neighborhood and she knew where they hid the spare key. She also knew the code for their security system. Every year she was given strict orders to check on their plants while they were away. The Millers had no children and couldn't tolerate pets. Their plants were their babies. She'd stopped by before leaving for Chicago. This was the perfect place to go now. If any of the neighbors saw her they wouldn't suspect a thing.

Sam seemed to be sleeping by the time she pulled into the Millers' driveway. She parked the rental on the other side of the garage in the spot where the Winnebago usually sat. The rental wouldn't be visible from the street, and Chuck had no reason to think she would come here. As far as she could recall she'd never mentioned the Millers to him.

With the drugstore bag in hand she retrieved the spare key from its hiding place in a magnetic holder beneath the elbow in the gutter downspout. Leaving Sam in the car until she'd opened the door and disarmed the security system, she checked to make sure all was as it should be inside. Then she went back for him.

"I'm not asleep," he muttered as she touched his shoulder. "I'm concentrating." He groaned as he pushed out of the seat. "Trying to block the pain until these pain relievers kick in."

She kept one arm around his waist as she guided him inside, then locked the door and reactivated the security system. "Do you want to go straight to bed after we've cleaned up your face?"

"Hot bath," he said on a grunt. "I think that and about four more of those pills might help."

There was a whirlpool tub in the master bath. She headed in that direction. He leaned against the counter and cleaned up his face with a damp cloth while she prepared the water in the tub. He swore repeatedly as he worked. She winced each time she glanced his way. One eye was swollen almost to the point of being closed. The other wasn't quite so bad but couldn't be called good.

When she'd gotten the hot water to the required level, she stood, bumped the bowl of bath crystals, knocking it into the water. "Damn!" She grabbed it, but it was too late. "Looks like you're going to have a bubble bath," she said wearily.

He tried to smile and grimaced. "No problem. I love bubble baths."

As tired as she was, she laughed. "Whatever. Get in the tub. I'll get you some ice."

On her way to the kitchen, she slowed to admire the gorgeous view from the wall of windows and French doors that extended the length of the back of the house. The pool glistened invitingly beyond those French doors. The furnishings were modern yet elegant. Seemed weird to be hiding from the cops in such a posh environment.

In the kitchen she turned on the news while she prepared an ice bag for Sam's swollen eyes. There wasn't any change in what was being reported on the news about the shooting incident. The whole idea was crazy. They hadn't been anywhere near Fiftieth tonight, and there definitely hadn't been any shoot-outs in the neighborhood they'd visited.

She thought of Sam, out cold lying on the floor of that leased building, and the missing weapons.

That was it. Someone had followed them there and waited for the right moment to take the weapons. She would bet her life that the weapons had been used or planted at the scene of the shootings being reported. Her own partner was framing her. She couldn't be certain that was the case, but her instincts were screaming at her to consider the possibility. It would take some fancy footwork to clear that up. Some stupid part of her still didn't want to believe that her partner was the one…but he was. There was no doubt about it now.

She could get kicked off the force because of him, could go to prison.

Could get dead.

Tomorrow's plan had to work. That was the only way out of this whole mess.

The bottle of blush wine in the refrigerator lured her attention back there when she would have closed the door. She could definitely use a drink. And since the pain reliever wasn't the kind that warned against the use of alcohol in conjunction with it, Sam could have one, too.

With two stemmed glasses in one hand, the bottle and the ice bag in the other, she shuffled back to the master suite. She tucked the bottle under one arm and tapped the door.

"Are you in the tub? Can I come in?"

"Yes on both counts."

A trail of clothes led from the sink to the tub. Jeans…socks…shirt…boxers…and then Sam, neck deep in hot water and bubbles in that huge tub.

She placed the glasses on the deck of the tub, then set the bottle of wine there. "Here." She handed him the bag of ice. "That should help the swelling."

"Thanks." He pressed the bag to the eye that was so painfully swollen. He grimaced at the contact.

"Could you use a glass of wine?"

"No." He looked at her with his good eye. "I want at least three."

"No problem. There's plenty more where this came from." She filled his glass and handed it to him. "The Millers have a great wine cellar."

"How long are they going to be gone?"

"For another week." She poured her own glass of wine and sipped it, relishing the smooth taste and the promise of relaxation.

"We could drink a lot of wine and take a lot of bubble baths in a week."

Another of those real smiles spread across her lips. "You're right. We could."

Deciding that sipping her wine wasn't getting the job done, she downed most of the glass. Then poured another. When she'd polished off the better part of it, she poured Sam another and said, "I think I'll have a shower."

"Leave the wine here," he ordered. "I need it worse than you do."

He was right about that, in part anyway.

The shower was in a smaller room along with the toilet. She badly needed a shower anyway and sitting there amid all that rising steam with images of what Sam Johnson looked like under all those bubbles was more than she could tolerate.

She washed her hair then turned the water to the

hottest setting she could bear. Slowly her muscles started to relax and the worries of the day faded just a little. By the time the water had started to cool, she felt tremendously better. After toweling her hair and drying her body, she donned the plush robe hanging on the back of the door.

"Is it okay to come out?" she called through the door before stepping out into the part of the bathroom where she'd left Sam bathing.

No answer. Maybe he'd already finished his bath and retired to the bedroom.

She cracked the door open and peeked out, didn't see him so she emerged. He'd drained the tub, even rinsed it and found a robe or something to put on since his clothes were still strewn over the floor. She gathered his discarded attire and placed everything in a neat pile on the counter. Then she went in search of him.

Sam had found his way to the kitchen and was preparing a cheese and fruit tray when Lisa surfaced from her long shower. He felt immensely better, but he was going to be as sore as hell come morning.

"You hungry?" he asked her.

"Not really, but considering how much wine I've had I'd better eat something."

They claimed seats at the island and had another glass of wine along with the cheese and grapes.

"Do you think Watts went for our story?"

"I'm certain he did." She glanced at the muted television. "I don't know how this will affect his decision to show. We'll just have to wait and see. Plain old curiosity may bring him to the rendezvous point."

"That's assuming those guys who roughed me up weren't part of Watts's crew and somehow knew what we were up to."

She sighed. "Yeah. I thought about that. But how could they have known?"

"Don't know." He popped a grape into his mouth. "Anders called while you were delivering your message. He said that the guys Houston sent confirmed delivery of the message to Sanford." Sam had touched base with him while Lisa showered to let him know they were safe and to ensure he could still track their location with the microfiber bugs they both wore. Anders had assured him all was a go.

"So Sanford thinks Lil Watts is meeting with a new LAPD contact at noon tomorrow in hopes of trading him in for a better model."

"Right. No matter what happens tonight, I don't think he'll be able to resist putting in an appearance just to see what's going down."

Lisa nibbled on her cheese. "God, I hope so. I'm so tired of all this craziness."

Sam pushed off the stool. "Why don't we take this to the bedroom and relax?"

"Good idea."

By the time they'd transported their booty to the master bedroom, it hit Sam that sharing a bed with Lisa was going to do many things, but relaxing him wasn't one of them.

"Why don't you take this room?" he suggested, "and I'll find another." With a house this big there was bound to be a number of bedrooms.

"No." She set the bottle of wine and the glasses on the bedside table. "I want you with me."

He placed the platter on the table on his side of the king-size bed. "It's a big bed. I think we can manage."

"I think so," she echoed.

Together they pulled the covers back. He groaned, this time with something besides pain, as he settled onto the cool sheets. The bed felt heavenly and the cool sheets reminded him just how tired he was.

"You think we'll find our way out of this?" she asked in a small voice.

She was scared. She would never admit it, but she was.

"Maybe. Yes."

Silence.

"I'm sorry I ever thought you might be involved with those murders. I was wrong." She exhaled a big, weary breath. "About a lot of things."

Knowing it was going to hurt like hell, he rolled to his side so he could look at her. "We were both wrong about a lot of things. We're human. Don't beat yourself up over any of this. You wanted to believe the best in your partner. You couldn't have known what he was doing. Hell, evidently, no one does."

She rolled toward him. "You're right."

Her blond hair was still damp, but the way it fell across her throat made him want to reach out and touch her there. She was so beautiful. Big brown eyes and peach-colored lips that looked more kissable than any he'd ever seen. Tasted that way, too, he acknowledged, remembering that brief kiss they'd shared.

As if she'd been thinking about that moment, too, she said, "I'm glad you kissed me tonight. It was nice."

Nice. Not exactly what he'd been going for.

"I'll try to do better next time." He laughed softly, but his attention was riveted to that mouth, already wishing for the opportunity to do better than "nice."

"You could try to do better now," she offered.

Heat rushed along his limbs, hardening every muscle in his body in an instant. "You talked me into it." He leaned his head closer, pressed his lips to hers.

The kiss was tentative at first. Slow and easy. No need to rush. Not like before. There was no hurry. The fingers of her right hand gingerly touched his jaw, taking care not to delve into damaged territory. The feel of her fingers against his skin set him on fire. He wasn't sure how much of that he could take.

He touched her next. First her throat…then her breast. Together, taking their time, they released the ties of each other's robe. The exploration took his breath away, made him crazy with want for her. She touched him everywhere, tenderly, making him forget all about the pain. Not letting her get ahead of him, he examined every inch of her—could scarcely catch his breath between kisses.

She rolled onto her back and urged him to move on top of her. Their bodies fit together perfectly. They cried out together as he sank slowly, deeply inside her. The heat, the sensations…all of it pushed him closer and closer to an edge he hadn't visited in so long.

They found release together, then collapsed, tangled in a damp, hot heap. Long minutes later, when their respirations had slowed to somewhere near normal, they indulged in more wine and cheese and then the kissing started again. This time the lovemaking was more frantic…more desperate.

And this time they drifted off to sleep wrapped in each other's arms after coming apart so completely that Sam wasn't sure he would ever be the same again.

Chapter Fourteen

"If just one thing goes wrong," Victoria warned, "Sam and Lisa could both end up dead. Not to mention Detective Sanford and Lil Watts and his followers."

Jim strove for patience, but it wasn't easy. "I'm very much aware of that, Victoria." If half of what he suspected about Sanford was true, he wasn't particularly worried about whether he ended up dead or not.

His mother crossed to the window that looked out on the park across the street from the brownstone the Equalizers called home. Jim was a little surprised to find Victoria waiting for him when he arrived at work that morning. Especially after the way they'd left things the last time they talked.

Victoria didn't agree with the strategy Johnson,

Anders and Jim had decided upon. She felt there was too much room for error. Too many things could go wrong.

It was the only way.

"I have a contact in California's State Bureau of Investigations," Jim went on when she didn't say more. "He's meeting with LAPD's Internal Affairs this morning to try and get a formal investigation going. We've covered every base possible in an effort to ensure the least amount of collateral damage."

Victoria turned back to him. "Then why can't this sting operation fall under IA's jurisdiction or CBI? Why risk this rogue attempt?"

Jim braced his hands against his desk and fixed the firmest glare he could on his mother. "Because we don't have the luxury of time. IA won't do anything until they have justifiable cause—evidence. The word of a gang lord is hardly that. We have to do this now before anyone involved can cover his tracks."

"It's too dangerous." She crossed her arms over her chest, unconvinced. "I could speak to Lucas. See what he could do to hasten things along."

Lucas Camp, Jim's stepfather, was connected, that was for certain. CIA, Homeland Security, you name it. But time simply wouldn't allow a deviation from the plan already in place.

"Mother," Jim said for emphasis, "there are

hundreds—no thousands—of gang members on those streets. Right now there is a contract on Sam Johnson. It's a miracle he's survived the past forty-eight hours in L.A. I'm not risking his life another night. This has to go down today."

"You know that any taped evidence they collect in this operation won't be admissible in court," she reminded, the wheels in her head working overtime to come up with a way to stop this sting from going down.

"Yes, I know. But what it will do is prove what Charles Sanford has been up to. My guess is he'll be trying to cut a deal so fast IA won't know what hit them."

Victoria closed her eyes a moment, her demeanor uncharacteristically troubled. "There are a dozen things that could go wrong."

"You're right. We've moved Johnson's family to a private safe house. Battles and Call will be working with Anders behind the scenes."

"That's a decision I should have been in on," Victoria reminded, disappointment flashing in her eyes.

Jim straightened. "You mean the way I was in on the decision to brief the Johnson family about Sam's presence in California?"

She didn't respond at first. Jim took that opportunity to say something he'd been holding back for a while now. "You're going to have to let me make my own mistakes, Victoria. It's the only way I can move on with my future."

Victoria walked to his desk, held his gaze with those dark eyes. "Even when I know the consequences are grave?"

"Even when you know I'll fail," he confirmed. "This is my life now. You have to allow me to live it."

She reached for her purse and squared her shoulders. "I suppose there's nothing else I can say."

"Not about this operation, no."

"I'll urge my investigators to cooperate fully with Spencer since change at the eleventh hour would only work against us all. But understand that I disagree wholly with this operation. Sometimes playing by the rules *is* the best way to get the job done."

Victoria walked out of his office showing the same determination she'd had when she'd entered. Nothing he had said had altered her opinion of the situation one iota.

Was she right? Could he be risking too much? He and Anders had gone over the strategy for this operation a dozen times. This was the only way to force Sanford's hand. Johnson and Smith agreed. There simply was no alternative. Every minute brought the possibility of death closer to Sam Johnson. He was living on borrowed time.

It was all or nothing.

Jim just wished that Victoria had more faith in him. This didn't have to be a contest about who was the better strategist or who had the most experience. This whole thing felt like a war of blood against blood, Colby against Colby.

The Equalizers were off to a great start. He needed Victoria to recognize that and to respect it.

To respect him as an equal.

Chapter Fifteen

"It's the only way," Sam argued.

Lisa had to walk away. She couldn't listen to any more of this. Sam Johnson was intent on getting himself killed. The man would not listen to reason.

They'd taken up their position at Soupy's, an out-of-business soup kitchen that had served the community for more than a decade before being abandoned because of the growing gang-related activities in the area.

Anders threw his hands up, as disgusted with Johnson as Lisa was. "Okay, man, it's your call."

Jeff Battles and Brett Call were playing lookout on the roof of the dry cleaner across the street. Jim Colby's contact at the California Bureau of Investigations was standing by as unofficial backup. They couldn't risk any official involvement for fear that a leak to LAPD would tip off Sanford. Most of the cops on the force were damned good men and women, but, like Lisa, no one would want to believe Sanford had crossed over to the dark side. Someone would tip him off out of respect.

Considering they were basically on their own, the danger to all involved was multiplied many times over, but there was no help for it. Even if they dared risk involving other cops or anyone from CBI, another gun was the last thing they were going to need; paramedics and maybe a miracle, considering Sam Johnson's inflexible attitude.

She had spent the morning with Anders and Sam rigging the place for video and audio surveillance. Whatever went down in here today would be recorded, so there would be no changing of stories.

The down side to that was that none of the recorded material would be admissible in court *unless* one participant in the conversation and/or activities had consented. Sam wanted to be that someone, putting himself directly in the line of fire.

Lisa wanted to shake him. Actually she wanted to punch him. She closed her eyes and recalled the way they'd made love last night. Every touch… every whispered word had claimed a place in her heart. How the hell could she let him do this?

If he'd been planning to get himself killed, he

had no business making her fall in love with him. Damn it!

"It's time," Anders said.

Final preparations had to be made.

Lisa took a deep breath and did what she had to do.

She and Anders had rigged a surveillance cubicle from the walk-in cooler that was more a hot box than a cooler since there was no electricity. They'd drilled holes leading into the main rooms of the establishment and run video and audio feeds to each. Their weapons were already inside the makeshift safe room. Since cell phones wouldn't work in the cooler, Anders had engineered a landline by tying in to the phone line used by the restaurant across the alley. The restaurant didn't open until four so there wouldn't be any problem with keeping that line open between them and Battles and Call. Vernon Street flanked Soupy's on the other side. The CBI contact had taken a position in a surveillance van on the other side of Vernon.

Sam would stay out of sight in a janitor's closet in a corridor just off the main room. He would enter the scene after the others were on-site while Lisa and Anders monitored the equipment and called in backup if needed.

All three wore body armor, which made for some major perspiration issues…not counting the way her heart and pulse were racing with worry for Sam.

One wrong move, one misunderstanding could cause this thing to turn into a blood bath. But then, she'd done something similar last night and had been just as adamant that Sam allow her to do what had to be done. She had no room to complain today. But she did just the same.

Sam's face was pretty battered, he had matching shiners, but most of the swelling had gone down thanks to the ice. He was sore as hell. He didn't have to say so, the grimace he made with every move told the tale all on its own.

Lisa walked up to Sam, braced her hands on her hips and gave him a glare that said just how ticked off she was. "Try not to get yourself killed, will ya?"

A smile tugged at the corners of his mouth and he winced. "I'll see what I can do."

She started to turn away, since she knew Anders was waiting, but she hesitated. "He's my partner, you know," she said to Sam. "It really should be me out here."

Sam shook his head. "Nope. This is my problem. I'm going to fix it. I want this over so…" That gray gaze caressed hers with a tender look. "So I can get on with my life."

It was stupid, she knew, but she couldn't stop herself. She grabbed him by the ears and pulled his mouth down to hers. The kiss was soft in deference to his sore lips and lasted all of ten seconds, but every moment touched her in a way nothing else ever had.

She drew back, searched his eyes one last time, then walked away. Anders waited for her in the kitchen.

"Ladies first." He gestured to the cooler door.

Unable to speak for fear of letting her foolish emotions show, she jerked the door open and went inside. Anders had set up battery-operated lanterns. She had to give the man credit, he knew how to set up an op in the most challenging of situations.

He closed the cooler door and dropped the steel bar into place that would prevent anyone from being able to open the door from the outside. Lisa tucked her communications earpiece into place.

The players could show up at any time even though they had a half hour before the arranged meeting time.

Lisa watched on the monitor as Sam disappeared into the closet.

"I've got two dark SUVs arriving," Battles related via the communications link.

Lisa braced.

"SUVs are moving on," Battles confirmed. From his position on that rooftop he could see trouble coming from quite a distance.

She made a conscious effort to relax, focused on keeping the tension at bay. She had to be ready for anything and at the same time thinking clearly and calmly. Some tension was good, but too much could screw up the best training.

"We have movement on Vernon," Call said, the words filtering across the link. "It's the same two black SUVs," he verified.

"They've parked at your Twenty," Battles confirmed the stop in front of Soupy's. "Four subjects emerging from each vehicle. Eight total. They'll be inside in five…four…three…the door is opening… they're inside."

"We have the subjects on our monitors," Anders said quietly. That was another handy thing about the cooler—soundproof.

"Lil Watts is present and accounted for," Lisa confirmed for all listening, including the CBI contact who was tied in to their communications link. Sam's visual was limited from his position. Keeping him up to speed audibly was essential.

Watts ordered three of his men to move to the rear of the building, which meant the kitchen. One was sent back out to cover the sidewalk. The others stayed inside with Watts. He wasn't about to be caught without a number of bodyguards, all armed for war.

"We have movement in the alley," Battles stated. "Three—no four subjects."

More of that bad tension rippled through Lisa.

"I have visual confirmation on Sanford." This from Call.

Lisa had been telling herself all night that she was prepared for this, but the reality that her partner was indeed dirty shocked her all over again.

She'd worked with him for five years. Respected and admired him. Not once had she seen anything out of him that wasn't by the book. And here she stood waiting to watch him meet with the man who committed heinous crimes on his orders. She wasn't sure she would ever get accustomed to the idea.

"It's 'bout time," Watts groused as he watched out the window, evidently catching sight of Sanford and his pals.

The four men entered what had once been a dining room. Sanford, Hernandez, Wallingsford and Edmonds. All veteran detectives in Priority Homicide.

Unbelievable.

"What the hell's this about, Watts?" Sanford demanded. He looked around, expecting to find whoever Watts was supposed to meet.

Watts went toe to toe with him. "What you asking me for? You're the one who set up this party."

Lisa watched realization dawn on Sanford's face. "What the hell are you talking about?"

"Your partner said you wanted to meet," Watts sneered. "She said you had plans to switch your loyalty to the other side and I ain't having none of that."

Sanford glanced around the room. "She's playing you, you idiot. She's probably here somewhere taping this whole damned thing."

"She was pretty convincing, dog," Watts warned. "I think maybe I rather believe her than believe you."

"Shut up," Sanford commanded. He jerked his head as a signal to his cohorts. The three detectives fanned out, moving into the other parts of the building looking for Lisa and Sam no doubt.

The door to the cooler jerked a couple of times, but the would-be-intruder moved on, evidently assuming it was locked and empty.

Lisa and Anders exchanged a look.

"You been talking to Buster?" Watts demanded of Sanford. "Your partner says you made a deal with him."

"I said shut up," Sanford ordered.

"You hear that?" Watts said to one of his cronies. "He wants me to shut up."

Movement in the corridor caused Lisa's breath to catch. Sam entered the room from the side corridor. Weapons were swung in his direction.

"Why don't you tell him the truth, Sanford," Sam suggested. "You may think he's just a dumb punk, but he's pretty smart."

Watts glared at Sanford. "What the hell is he doing here?" He looked at the men on either side of him. "He shouldn't even still be alive. Somebody's falling behind on their work."

Lisa wanted to go out there. As if sensing her anticipation, Anders moved up beside her. "Let's just stay calm and focused."

"You've been made, Sanford," Sam said to Lisa's partner. "And you're all going down with him," he said with a glance at each detective as they reentered the room.

"This is your mess," Sanford said to Watts. "You clean it up."

"You," Watts snarled at Sam, "are a dead man."

"So everyone keeps saying," he muttered.

Watts pulled out his .40 caliber and shoved it against Sam's chest. "If a man wants something done right he just has to do it himself."

Lisa grabbed her weapon and started for the door. Anders grabbed her arm. "Not yet."

"Don't trouble yourself," Lisa heard Sanford say, and went back to the monitor. "He and Smith are both going down for murder. Their prints were found on the murder weapons at the scene of a shooting last evening. I'll just take Johnson into custody and that'll be the end of that."

"Are you crazy?" Watts demanded. "I want this bastard dead. For good. I'm sick of him showing up.

My uncle was stupid enough to make a deal with him. I don't do business with fools like him."

"Just calm down, Watts," Sanford urged. "We can handle this. Whatever's going on, it's contained in this building. Johnson tried to set us both up. But we don't have to worry. He's a killer." Sanford stared at Sam as he said this. "It's time he did the time for his crimes."

Lisa's pulse raced. This could go so wrong any second. The whole game was being held together by a single thread—Sam Johnson.

"Actually," Sam said, "it's you who needs to do time, Detective Sanford." Sam gestured to Watts. "Tell him how you've been using him to do your dirty work. When you wanted someone out of the way, you ordered Watts to have some of his people do it so the deed would be written off as more gang violence. All you had to do was look the other way when Watts had business of his own to carry out without the worry of being caught and prosecuted. Seemed like a fair deal for everybody."

Sanford laughed, the sound grated on Lisa's nerves.

"You're speculating, Johnson. You should know by now that the only thing that counts is evidence. And you don't have a shred of evidence to support what you're alleging. So let's cut to the chase." He nodded, and Hernandez stepped forward. "You have the right to remain silent…."

Hernandez jerked Sam's hands behind his back to restrain him with nylon cuffs.

"Ask Buster," Sam said to Watts, ignoring Hernandez. "He has pictures to back up his stories. Sanford is playing you. Three cops in as many years." Sam shook his head. "Somebody's going to have to pay for real, eventually. He's staging the battlefield for a war and you're going to be the first casualty."

Sanford backhanded him. "Shut. Up."

Lisa turned to Anders then. "That's it. I'm going out there before this thing gets out of control."

"Let him go."

Everyone in the room pivoted to stare at the man standing in the entrance. Lisa's jaw dropped.

Buster Houston.

"What the hell is he doing here?" she murmured.

"Beats the hell out of me," Anders said, just as stunned.

"Clear the room, Watts," Buster commanded. "Just you, me, Johnson and Sanford. We're going to set the record straight."

Watts pointed his finger in the older man's face. "I got nothing to say to you, old man. Your people killed my uncle and you did nothing about it. I could have my vengeance right now with you showing up here like this. You must be going foolish for sure. If you had respected my uncle the way he respected you this thing would not have happened."

Houston stared at him for a second that turned into five. "When we're finished here, if you still feel I betrayed your uncle, then you can put a bullet in my skull and no one will retaliate. You have my word."

No less than a dozen—including those belonging to the three men who had followed Houston inside—weapons had leveled on targets. For ten or so trauma-filled seconds Lisa was certain Watts wouldn't do as Houston asked. Then, to her amazement, one slight flicker of his hand and the room cleared. Except for Hernandez, Edmonds and Wallingsford.

"No way am I sending my detectives out of this room," Sanford said. "We all stay."

Lisa leaned closer to the monitor, didn't want to miss a single facial expression.

When Watts didn't argue, Houston turned to Sanford. "You are a disgrace to your department. You are a disgrace to us all. And you are finished."

Lisa tensed. "Anders…" This was about to blow.

"Give it another minute," he urged as they watched the drama unfold.

Sanford laughed long and loud. "And just who the hell gave you the right to judge me, old man?"

"James Watts," Houston said. "You had him killed for your own selfish reasons, and for that you're going to pay."

Lil Watts looked from Houston to Sanford. "What's he talking 'bout?"

"He's a crazy old man who has outlived his purpose." Sanford pressed the barrel of his weapon to Houston's forehead. "But I can fix that right now."

"Don't you want to see the pictures?" Sam piped up, his expression a little frantic.

Lisa strained to see if that was panic on his face.

Watts demanded, "What pictures?" His voice was thick with suspicion.

Houston indicated his jacket pocket. "See for yourself," he said to Watts.

Sanford pivoted, swung his weapon toward Watts. Sam charged him.

The first shot exploded in the room.

"Now," Anders said as he headed for the door two steps in front of Lisa.

The silence that followed was even more deafening than the sound of bullets flying.

All four detectives and nearly a dozen gangsters faced off in the dilapidated dining room. The variety of weapons would have fascinated any arms dealer. Sam had Sanford pinned to the floor. Nobody moved.

Lisa and Anders stood on the fringes of the deadly standoff, weapons leveled on no one in particular.

Sam jerked Sanford's weapon out of his hand and got to his feet. Sanford scrambled up right next to him, glowering at him with murder in his eyes.

"So," Sam said as he looked around, the confiscated weapon hanging at his side, "how many are going to die here today?"

When no one answered, he went on, "Just so you know, this whole reality show has been recorded for the viewing pleasure of Internal Affairs and the District Attorney's office. We can all kill each other, or I can have some volunteers for plea bargains. What's it gonna be, boys?"

Wallingsford backed away a couple of steps and lowered his weapon. "I want a lawyer."

"Keep your mouth shut, you idiot!" Sanford shouted.

Hernandez lowered his weapon. "I want a deal."

Lisa felt a smile stretch across her lips. It was working.

"They're bluffing!" Sanford screamed.

"No." Lisa stepped forward, garnering herself some wary glances with her abrupt move. "We're not bluffing. At least three detectives are dead and there's no way to know how many others because of you," she said to Sanford. "You're the worst kind of scumbag. You even kill your own."

The move was so sudden and she was so angry that Lisa didn't see it coming. Sanford grabbed Hernandez's arm, swinging his weapon upward and jamming the man's finger against the trigger.

The sound exploded in the air. The bullet plowed into Lisa's chest, pitching her backward in a kind of slow motion. She slammed against the floor. Other weapons fired…but she couldn't see what was happening. She couldn't breathe…couldn't move.

And then Sam was on his knees next to her. "Lisa. God, are you okay?"

The air rushed into her lungs. She gasped. Coughed.

Her hands went to her chest. No blood. Relief flooded her.

"You're okay," Sam urged, pulling her up to lean against his chest. "The body armor," he reminded. "You're okay. God, you're okay."

She turned her head to see what the others were doing…but she couldn't see for all the people.

A uniformed man was suddenly hovering over her. Paramedic, she realized.

"Let's have a look, Detective Smith."

Things got a little confusing after that. But the one thing that Lisa could hang on to was Sam. He never left her side.

Chapter Sixteen

Sam closed the file on his own case.

It was finished.

Detectives Wallingsford and Hernandez had spilled their guts, and Sanford was going up the river for a very long time. Watts and Houston had managed plea bargains. Considering no one had died that day, the District Attorney's office was in a very giving mood.

Sam's family was safe and life was back to normal for him. In most ways, that is.

There were still a few questions where his future was concerned.

But considering he hadn't heard from Lisa in more than two weeks, he wasn't so sure if he even had anything other than this job to look forward to.

He shoved the file into a drawer and railed at

himself for all the self-pity. He had his family. He had his life back. Business was booming here at the home of the Equalizers. And he did love his work.

Might as well call it a day. He pushed out of his chair and went to the window. His gaze landed on Jim Colby sitting on the front step. Things were still a little tense between him and his mother. Sam wanted to tell the man that life was short and he shouldn't drag this thing out.

Looked like he wouldn't have to.

A car parked at the street and the driver emerged.

Victoria Colby-Camp.

A smile tugged at Sam's mouth. Oh, to be a fly on the step next to Jim.

Sam turned away from the window. Maybe he'd hang around and see how things turned out.

He wouldn't mind another happy ending.

"Victoria." Jim started to stand.

"Keep your seat," she insisted as she approached.

He watched her, this strong, independent woman who had survived hell on earth and still came out fighting. He loved her. The admission shook him a little. But it was true. He loved his mother fiercely.

Somehow they had to find neutral territory again.

She sat down on the step beside him. The image of her sitting on that stone step with her tailored suit and perfectly coiffed hair was something one didn't see every day, but that was Victoria. She set her own style, her own rhythm.

"It's time we ended this standoff."

He was all for that. "We could've done that weeks ago, if you'd chosen to be reasonable."

She cleared her throat delicately. "Reason isn't the issue, Jim."

Here they went again. "Yes, it is."

"Even Tasha—"

"Tasha isn't taking sides," he clarified before she could go there. He and his wife had had a long talk about her position on the matter. "She loves both of us and doesn't want to be put in the middle. Just because she doesn't argue with your point of view doesn't mean she agrees 100 percent, any more than she does with mine."

"You know I only want the best for you. I've waited a very long time to see you happy."

The reminder made his gut clench. "I know that. But we have to learn to respect each other's boundaries."

She laughed softly. "You know what this sounds like, don't you? It's like we're living all the things we missed, the rebellious years of adolescence, the growing pains of early adulthood, all in one big complicated lump of frustrating episodes."

Her vulnerable sincerity as much as her words made him smile. "I think you're right. That's how it feels. I need my space and you want to protect me, like I was sixteen instead of twenty-eight."

"I'm sorry, Jim." She sighed, the sound heavy-hearted. "I've overstepped my bounds repeatedly and I'm not sure how to make it right."

"Mother."

She faced him, her dark eyes too bright.

"Maybe the fact that I had a problem saying this out loud has been part of the problem, but *I love you*." His throat tightened with emotion. "Deep down I've always loved you even when I thought I hated you. I know you want the best for me. That you want to protect me. But you don't need to be afraid for me. You need to trust me to be the man you believe I can be."

A smile trembled across her lips. "Well said, son. I think that's exactly what I need to do."

They hugged, something they didn't do enough.

And that was the end of the standoff. No more Colby versus Colby. From now on, they would stand together as equals. Unstoppable forces. The Colby Agency and the Equalizers.

"Excuse me."

Jim looked up, as did Victoria.

Lisa Smith stood on the walkway. "I'm sorry to interrupt."

Jim stood, extended his hand. "No problem. How have you been?"

She smiled. "I've been good."

Victoria dabbed at her eyes and produced a smile. "What brings you to Chicago, Lisa?"

As if his mother didn't know. Jim kept that thought to himself.

"Is Sam here?" Lisa asked, her expression hopeful.

Jim hitched a thumb toward the door. "You're in luck. He's still hanging around. Probably waiting to hear if Victoria and I worked things out."

Lisa looked from him to Victoria and back. "Well…did you?"

"We did," Victoria assured her. "We found that place we've been looking for." She looked up at Jim, her face beaming. "Common ground."

"That's great. Really great." Lisa gestured to the door. "I'll give Sam the good news." Lisa flashed a smile for Jim and his mother, then hurried up the steps and into the office.

Connie Gardner looked up from her computer. "We're closed," she said grumpily.

Biting back a chuckle, Lisa assured her, "Yeah, I know. I'm here to see Sam."

"He's in his office," Connie said without looking up again from her work.

When Lisa hesitated, the receptionist gestured to a hall beyond her desk and to the left. "His office is the second door on the left."

"Thanks." Lisa took a deep breath and headed that way. She hesitated outside his closed door and smoothed her palms over her skirt. She'd fretted over what she would wear today as if she'd been dressing for senior prom.

It was silly, she knew, but she just couldn't help herself.

She squared her shoulders and knocked.

The door opened and Sam was standing there. His mouth opened, but the words didn't come for a second.

"Lisa."

"May I come in?"

"Oh…yeah." He stepped back, opened the door wider. "I was just packing up for the day."

"I would have been here sooner, but my flight was delayed."

Sam looked confused. He indicated a chair in front of his desk. "Please have a seat."

She didn't want to sit. She wanted to throw her arms around him and kiss him…she wanted to sweep his desk clean and make love to him right there.

Clearing her mind, she recalled the script she'd mentally written.

"I'm actually looking for a job."

He looked surprised. "Oh. So you're giving up police work?"

She dropped her purse into the chair he'd offered. "I was hoping the Equalizers needed another associate."

"You want to work here?" He pointed to the floor, his expression shifting from surprised to shocked.

She nodded. "I'm looking for an apartment, too. If you have any suggestions, that would be great."

"You're moving here? To Chicago?"

Lisa had to smile. Obviously her revelation had startled him to the point he was having trouble thinking straight. She hoped that was a good thing.

"Do you have a problem with that?"

He shook his head adamantly. "No. No way. I'm thrilled to hear it."

"Good." She couldn't take it anymore. She reached for him, flattened her palms on that muscular chest. "Because I'm looking for a long-term relationship, too."

The shock on his face melted into a goofy, satisfied smile. "I was sure hoping you'd say that."

She moved in closer, lifted her arms up around his neck. "I had to work things out, Sam. Had to make sure I didn't leave any loose ends back in L.A."

"I understand." His arms went around her. "As you recall, I had a few of those I had to take care of myself."

Now, that was something she wouldn't be soon forgetting.

"So, do you think your boss would be interested in a former homicide detective?"

"I'm sure he will be very interested." Sam pulled her more firmly against him. "And I have this great place with space to spare so you won't be needing an apartment."

"What about the long-term relationship thing?" It was all or nothing. She wasn't wasting any more time.

"How does forever sound?"

"Forever is good."

He kissed her lips, just the softest brush of his.

"Then you got it," he murmured.

She went up on tiptoe and kissed him the way she'd been dying to since the last time they kissed. This was worth all the hell they had gone through. Worth the world.

Nothing could stop them now.

* * * * *

*Watch for the return of the Colby Agency
in November 2007 from Debra Webb
and Harlequin Intrigue.*

THE ROYAL HOUSE OF NIROLI
Always passionate, always proud

The richest royal family in the world—united by blood and passion, torn apart by deceit and desire.

Nestled in the azure-blue of the Mediterranean Sea, the majestic island of Niroli has prospered for centuries. The Fierezza men have worn the crown with passion and pride since ancient times. But now, as the king's health declines, and his two sons have been tragically killed, the crown is in jeopardy.

The clock is ticking—a new heir must be found before the king is forced to abdicate. By royal decree the internationally scattered members of the Fierezza family are summoned to claim their destiny. But any person who takes the throne must do so according to The Rules of the Royal House of Niroli. Soon secrets and rivalries emerge as the descendents of this ancient royal line vie for position and power. Only a true Fierezza can become ruler—a person dedicated to their country, their people…and their eternal love!

Each month starting in July 2007,
Harlequin Presents is delighted to bring you
an exciting installment from
THE ROYAL HOUSE OF NIROLI,
in which you can follow the epic search
for the true Nirolian king.
Eight heirs, eight romances, eight fantastic stories!

Here's your chance to enjoy a sneak preview of the first book delivered to you by royal decree….

FIVE minutes later she was standing immobile in front of the study's window, her original purpose of coming in forgotten, as she stared in shocked horror at the envelope she was holding. Waves of heat followed by icy chill surged through her body. She could hardly see the address now through her blurred vision, but the crest on its left-hand front corner stood out, its *royal* crest, followed by the address: *HRH Prince Marco of Niroli...*

She didn't hear Marco's key in the apartment door, she didn't even hear him calling out her name. Her shock was so great that nothing could penetrate it. It encased her in a kind of bubble, which only concentrated the torment of what she was suffering and branded it on her brain so that it could never be forgotten. It was only finally pierced by the sudden opening of the study door as Marco walked in.

"Welcome home, *Your Highness*. I suppose I

ought to curtsy." She waited, praying that he would laugh and tell her that she had got it all wrong, that the envelope she was holding, addressing him as Prince Marco of Niroli, was some silly mistake. But like a tiny candle flame shivering vulnerably in the dark, her hope trembled fearfully. And then the look in Marco's eyes extinguished it as cruelly as a hand placed callously over a dying person's face to stem their last breath.

"Give that to me," he demanded, taking the envelope from her.

"It's too late, Marco," Emily told him brokenly. "I know the truth now…." She dug her teeth in her lower lip to try to force back her own pain.

"You had no right to go through my desk," Marco shot back at her furiously, full of loathing at being caught off-guard and forced into a position in which he was in the wrong, making him determined to find something he could accuse Emily of. "I trusted you…."

Emily could hardly believe what she was hearing. "No, you didn't trust me, Marco, and you didn't trust me because you knew that I couldn't trust you. And you knew that because you're a liar, and liars don't trust people because they know that they themselves cannot be trusted." She not only felt sick, she also felt as though she could hardly breathe. "You are Prince Marco of Niroli…. How could you not tell me who you are and still live with me as intimately as we have lived together?" she demanded brokenly.

"Stop being so ridiculously dramatic," Marco demanded fiercely. "You are making too much of the situation."

"*Too much?*" Emily almost screamed the words at him. "When were you going to tell me, Marco? Perhaps you just planned to walk away without telling me anything? After all, what do my feelings matter to you?"

"Of course they matter." Marco stopped her sharply. "And it was in part to protect them, and you, that I decided not to inform you when my grandfather first announced that he intended to step down from the throne and hand it on to me."

"To protect me?" Emily nearly choked on her fury. "Hand on the throne? No wonder you told me when you first took me to bed that all you wanted was sex. You *knew* that was the only kind of relationship there could ever be between us! You *knew* that one day you would be Niroli's king. No doubt you are expected to marry a princess. Is she picked out for you already, your *royal* bride?"

* * * * *

Look for
THE FUTURE KING'S PREGNANT MISTRESS
by Penny Jordan in July 2007,
from Harlequin Presents,
available wherever books are sold.